Stagg and his Mother

Stagg and his Mother

DAVID POWNALL

LONDON
VICTOR GOLLANCZ LTD
1991

First published in Great Britain 1991
by Victor Gollancz Ltd
14 Henrietta Street, London WC2E 8QJ

British Library Cataloguing in Publication Data
Pownall, David, *1938–*
    Stagg and his mother.
    I. Title
    823.914 [F]

ISBN 0-575-05032-2

Typeset at The Spartan Press Ltd,
Lymington, Hants
and printed in Great Britain by
St Edmundsbury Press Ltd, Bury St Edmunds, Suffolk

For my brother

She looked as if she sat by Eden's door,
and grieved for those who could return no more.

lines from Canto XV of *Don Juan* by Byron.

Chapter One

Malcolm Stagg lay on his bed and watched the clouds sail over from the eastern sea. Through the curved polaroid windows of his bedroom tower he saw them as white vessels full of old imaginings, a numinous navy blown by a wind which he knew was cold. Downstairs was his mother, recently arrived to stay at his house, perhaps until death, a woman newly shaken by thoughts and ideas, a spirit freshly disturbed at the roots, a mind long transfixed which was pulling free from the nails which had held it in place. Last night she had talked for five hours, keeping Stagg up long past his usual bedtime oblivious to his hints and yawns as he tried to convey to her his desire for sleep, unable to resist the flow of her own thoughts.

"Do you think Stalin came up from Hell, ready made?" she had said, banging the arm of the chair with her fist. "Of course he didn't! He was created by human beings, like us. We let him get born. We made him like the cook made the gingerbread man."

Late as it was, Stagg had been forced to protest. Much as he loved his mother and was glad that her onrush of intellectual activity had come upon her at such an unexpected time — she was beyond seventy — he could not accept everything which she proposed in argument. He had told her that it was his view that Stalin had been the product of a certain type of political machine which ran on fossilised ideology and was still powering half of the globe.

"Never!" his mother had exhorted him. "You were responsible. As a little boy, you made him, and I made him, and that old buffer Churchill made him, the Queen made him. We were his ally. Everyone knew what he was up to in Russia but we didn't care because it wasn't in our back yard!" Here she had paused, her small hands nervously busy. Stagg had watched them, half-hypnotised, switching off as she continued with her harangue, his eyes getting heavier. "And another thing!" his mother had snapped, bringing him out of his doze. "All the world's countries will have to agree on a common history that they know is true, because I'm getting lost."

Stagg had nodded, aware of what she was going through: the dislocation and dismemberment of an entire lifetime's opinions, a kind of self-butchery, often wild and uncontrolled, which made him feel oddly proud that she should have such courage. Yet he could not help but be alarmed. If he had had a wife to assist him with Joyce, his mother, it would have been easier, even though he could not help but recall that not one of his three wives, nor any of his women friends, had ever won her approval. This did not discourage her from criticising him now for his treatment of them, nor from calling him a male chauvinist whenever it suited her to do so.

There was a tap at his door. Before he had time to answer it Joyce entered with a tea-tray. She was wearing a black track suit.

"Are you decent?" she said, plainly indifferent as to whether he was or not. "There's something I meant to say last night but I didn't have time because you were so anxious to get your beauty sleep." She sat down on the edge of the bed and started to pour him a cup of tea. "I don't go along with guilt. That's all in the past. But the future is what matters. You should think about that, son; sitting here in this modern house with all its contemporary features doesn't mean your mind is up to date. Architecture is essentially old-fashioned. There's only so much you can do with a house. Deep down it's only a hut, isn't it? Even Buckingham Palace is just a hut."

Stagg watched his mother's dentures as she spoke, his mind on the retreat. He had always been a little scared of his love for her, respecting the hardness of her life and the code of conduct which she had mined out of it. She had always been his moral superior and the source of his values, and when he finally managed to persuade her to come and live with him he had suffered some doubt. Would he be up to it? Could he live under her scrutiny? To have left her where she was had been one option, but once the metamorphosis had started and he had become intimately involved with the awakening of her mind, this was no longer possible. In the small flat at West Kirby on the Wirral peninsula, a dormitory town, she would have gone mad and torn herself and her sister apart. Cissy, the sister, was an anxious soul, much given to defensive simplicity and lamentation, and she lacked the nous to cope with the new being. During the first few months of her awakening Joyce had persecuted her to the point of tears many times, insisting on discussions which were far beyond either the interests or abilities of the unfortunate woman. It had worried Stagg to note that his mother was already writing long letters to her, stacks of books at her elbow, quotes from which she laboriously copied out in order to head off any counter-arguments her sister might make in reply.

Stagg was suddenly aware of a change in his mother's expression. It had softened. He stopped looking at the movement of her dentures, and smiled warily.

"I haven't given you time to wake up, have I, son?" she said, pressing the tea-cosy down over the pot. "To be more considerate is one of my many resolutions. I take too much for granted. What have you got to do today?"

Stagg told her that he had to go to London for a meeting.

"Who with?"

It was a long, complicated explanation, involving a contract with a Danish company. Joyce listened patiently. When Stagg began to find its telling tedious, Joyce insisted that he should continue nonetheless, claiming that she could not be bored.

"Not now, son. I have to confess that I've been bored a lot in my life. God help me, I have to own up that you yourself have bored me in the past, even as a baby. Not your fault at all. Mine. I was the one. So, go on. This deal sounds fascinating. Is an exchange rate insurance clause always a good idea?"

Stagg laboured on, doing his best to make the business sound interesting, aware that he was bored with it himself. His mother sat and listened, her eyes on the passing clouds and a thoughtful smile on her lips, nodding occasionally.

"So, in view of that, would you support the idea of a world currency, son?" she said once he had squeezed all the entertainment he could out of the financial details.

Stagg sighed audibly. As yet he had not been able to get up to go to the bathroom. He was unshaven, his hair was all over the place and he needed to urinate.

"Perhaps we could discuss that later on, Joyce?" he said with a half-hearted laugh. "That's a knotty one."

"It's obvious, surely? If currency is based on an agreed and accepted means of exchange then world trade must eventually lead to world currency. Why gold? What's gold? If everyone agrees with the blurb on the banknote then they can use it from New Guinea to Widnes, can't they?"

Stagg swung his feet off the bed and upset the tray, spilling tea over the duvet.

"Oh, Malcolm, you're such a clumsy boy! What's the matter with you? Haven't you got eyes in your head?" his mother snapped, whisking the duvet off the bed and hurrying towards the bathroom. "I'll have to put it in cold water straight away or we'll never get the stain out."

Comforted by this return to the past and the echoes of old rebukes, Stagg left his bedroom and went along the corridor to one of the other five bathrooms in the building.

It took twenty minutes of dogged diplomacy to prevent Joyce from coming to London with him. Since she had arrived in Norfolk, Stagg's mother had attempted to accompany him on all his business trips, giving as her reason her need to widen her horizons. He had weakened only once and that experience had settled him in his prejudice against the idea that maternalism and business could ever mix. He had taken her to Cambridge where he was due to meet college authorities about an extension to a laboratory block. He had rightly calculated that Joyce would be so taken up by the historical sights of the city that she would be glad to leave him alone to get on with his work. However, lunch proved to be his downfall. Upon learning that his mother was due to meet him at a restaurant near the college, and having business still to discuss with Stagg, the dean and bursar came to lunch and were interrogated by Joyce on the subject of pollution on Merseyside. As they belonged to a college specialising in astro-physical crystallography they got sensitive when the blame for the poisoning of Liverpool was put on intellectuals like themselves. It took Stagg weeks to repair the damage, including a concession on his charges which he was forced to make in order to keep the contract from going sour.

Her new liveliness, however, was a real source of pleasure to him and he was determined to nurture it all he could. For thirty years, most of his thinking maturity, he had suffered the division between them which his education had created and he had always resented it. They had both toiled to build bridges, only to see them break and plunge into the chasm of their separation. She had all the weapons when verbal combat began over their different lifestyles. Stagg could not openly criticise the frugal, pared-down existence which his mother practised as part of her protest against society's shams and hypocrisies, only imply that her shuttered vision was self-defeating. Sometimes he had managed to lure her out of her lair but a night with his friends in a restaurant or a visit to the theatre would be enough to confirm her view that his education had only heightened his mind by lowering his resistance to everything that was phoney. This toing and froing had gone on for years, a cycle of invitations, refusals, huffs, long silences, reunions and reconciliations, culminating in the construction of Hilbre which, he realised, had not been built for himself, but for her.

It had been an assault on his own roots, a tearing up of old blindness and grief, a shocking attack whereby he wielded this sickle-shaped house, brandishing it at the crabbed, suffering pride which had stifled her for so long. Not that she had been aware of this truth, nor had he while designing and building it, but on the day that she came down to be with him as he moved in, he realised what he had done and the power which she had. Her first reaction had been exactly what he had anticipated. For three days she had sat in fury, unable to eat, remonstrating with him. Finally she had left, going home four days before her week's stay had been due to end. She had intended this to be a declaration of her disgust. Stagg had seen her off at the station, his offer to drive her back across the width of the country having been rejected, and his farewell kiss on her cheek had been warm and forgiving because he knew that the ruse had worked. A slow-release catalyst had been implanted in his mother's mind. It would cause her much discomfort but she would have to respond.

"It's everything I've ever done," he had said to her, "why be surprised that it's not like anything else you've seen?"

"Son," she had seethed, "it's arrogant to put a monstrosity like that on the earth, and conceited to think that it's worth anything."

As he drove through the tall, stone gates and along the coast road he remembered how he had searched the country from end to end to find red rocks of the same hue as his old home to be foundations of the new, the colour of the Dee estuary's sandstone, a soft rock which was sculpted by the waves into smooth, erotic shapes. From his childhood he had visions of the languorous islands off the coast and the splendid sweep of stone into basins and cauldrons where tidewaters boiled. But once he had left the Wirral and its giant housing estates which had almost marched from side to side of the peninsula, he had never wanted to go back. But he had yearned for the stone, its colour and texture. From Cornwall to Cumbria he had searched the west coast, for he had to have the sea, but he had not found the right site. On the east coast he had roamed over the land at the mouth of the Tees where the Triassic sandstone was exposed, but it had not been flat enough. Stagg wanted a level landscape for his masterpiece. Eventually he compromised, choosing a site on the coast of Norfolk, just north of Great Yarmouth, and brought in the red rock from a Cheshire quarry, hundreds of lorry-loads of it, to build a horned moon in Mars' colours, branching into two glass towers looking out over field and shore to the sea, a house which welcomed the wind.

He had called his house Hilbre after two islands off the Wirral coast at West Kirby, Big and Little Hilbre, moving shapes in his memory. It had hurt him when the house had been roundly condemned as a modernistic monstrosity by the local paper and he had seen that word, Hilbre, sharing the abuse with himself. It was a sacred word to Stagg. Here, in East Anglia, it was the chime of another language.

Stagg frowned grimly. He had lied to his mother. The meeting in London was not with a Danish company at all but with representatives of the new federal government in East Germany. If he had told Joyce that this was the case she would have gone into a centrifugal spin of enthusiasm, her memory flinging out a lifetime's misconceptions, now seen as such, and only fit for disposal. The vacuum created by this ruthless abandonment of century-old prejudices seemed to be his to fill. He had the advantage of living and operating in these new times, dealing with people who were caught in vast currents of change. If he did not help his mother, who would? She had talked about going to university, and he had not discouraged this, but in his heart he knew that she would not be able to cope with the problems of being a student. Her nature was too fierce and puritanical in its way. This, he thought, was not untypical of student attitudes, but to carry off the status of age she would need some of its bearing and aplomb, and Joyce scorned these attributes. She was, and always had been, a girl: previously the girl had been hemmed in by the rigour of her stern upbringing and her class loyalty, but now that some god had touched her forehead and ignited her mind the girl had been liberated. Stagg suspected that should his mother go to university she would turn out to be the most rabid radical on the campus. However, it was not an idea which he had dismissed. If life at Hilbre became too difficult, his mother driving him mad in her hunger for knowledge and intellectual activity, university might be the only recourse left open.

As he came to the roundabout and the road to Norwich he glanced back and saw the glass towers twinkling in the spring light. He had built the house to save his self-esteem and beat off despair with himself after the collapse of his third marriage. It was a child he had built, a compensation for the barrenness of three women he had loved and lost. Now this child had another child within it like a Russian doll. The fact that she was now old did not subtract from the sum of her innocence but, to her wondering son, added to that most irritating of qualities.

He accelerated down the open road, the surge of the car's powerful engine pressing him back into the seat. As he checked the speed to a steady eighty-five he glanced into the driving-mirror and caught himself smiling out of a face which he had come to believe was graven into the mask of the careworn.

Whatever else he did that day, whatever good or bad, he would unpick the lie of the morning and tell Joyce that it had been East Germany he had been dealing with, and take the consequences.

Joyce sat in the enormous, sun-filled lounge with her fourth cup of tea on her lap and waited for Mrs Hankinson, the daily help. Within the daunting vaults and looming chambers of her son's house the radio and television seemed to have little authority. The only communication which succeeded was between live people. The design of each room forced conversation to the fore as a means of containing the forces of the strange geometry which Stagg had used: his house dictated terms between the conscious and incogitant space. In the bathroom Joyce had talked to herself, animated by the sight of the naked woman in the great mirrors, framed in shining metals and stained glass, employing words of comfort to the lean, lined creature with its grey hair and narrowed eyes, hunched below a whorled ceiling.

But although Hilbre never made her feel at ease, she did not dislike it. When Malcolm had been building the house she had joined every other person who was allowed sight of the drawings in scoffing at his concept. Once it was finished and she had paid her first visit, Joyce had returned to the Wirral, furious and sore at the gigantic waste of money and time. Shortly afterwards she had begun to suffer the rising peaks of intense mental stimulation which had kept her awake for days, driving her out of her flat on longer and longer walks, into libraries, bookshops, adult education classes, anything to feed the remorseless, painful hunger of her mind. Now, having bowed to that demand within, she felt in tune with the effects of Hilbre on her spirit. After all, it was her son who had created it. In some ways it was undoubtedly the work of her own womb, and it had got her going.

Mrs Hankinson's small blue car came up the drive, breaking the line of the horizon and the parallels of sea and shore. Joyce stood up and went into the kitchen, putting the cup and saucer on the side of the sink to be washed. It was an act of homage to her reborn persona to leave that cup for someone else to wash. Every instinct urged her to do Mrs Hankinson's work for her as the woman was not efficient or diligent, but Joyce resisted, contenting herself with a friendly jibe now and then, slipping these skilful thrusts in when natural pauses occurred in their discussions. As Mrs Hankinson moved about the house with vacuum cleaner, bucket and mop, brush and pan, polish and duster, Joyce was prone to follow her and in this she was encouraged. Mrs Hankinson was a lively mind herself, the wife of a hard-drinking, manic-depressive furniture-maker renowned for his idleness. She had married him during a romantic outburst, leaving her previous husband, a solicitor, to wither in sedate grief. By previous liaisons the Hankinsons had five children, all of whom had left home; nor could these children ever find time to summon up the energy to return and face the daily battle between the craftsman and his nerve-wracking muse.

"How are you today?" Mrs Hankinson said with a toss of her floppy black hair, her genteel but sparky voice crackling in an early eruption of spleen. "Don't ask me how I am, for God's sake. This head of mine, Joyce, I tell you, I'm at the end of my tether. He's completely ruined my day already." Then followed a detailed and lucid account of every action and reaction between herself and Alec, her husband, since waking that morning.

"Another bad start for you then, Moira?" Joyce said evenly.

"Disastrous, not that he cares!" came the reply.

Joyce nodded. She did not offer to pour her tea as that would have broken the standing rules of their relationship so far.

"Has Malcolm gone away? I noticed the tyre marks coming out of the puddles," Mrs Hankinson said, sitting down. "He never stops does he? All credit to him. He's done it all himself, worked his way up from nothing. Every time I come in this house I tell myself that. What a man. As you say, Joyce, he's made it out of his own head. Now, if I did that it would be like walking into the House of Horrors. What's this?" She picked up a slip of paper with *intussusception* written on it.

"It's Malcolm's word of the day for me," Joyce explained, "but I can't even pronounce it. He says it means 'taking in ideas'."

"Don't mention it to my husband then, if you ever meet him. He'd die of fright," Mrs Hankinson said rancorously. "Why do I stay with him? I can see the answer on your lips. But you're from an older generation, Joyce; we younger women have more pride, or we should have."

Mrs Hankinson paused to drink her tea, her wide lemur's eyes golden with indignation. Then she blinked and fell completely silent.

"Did you bring my newspapers?" Joyce asked after a while.

"Oh, God, I left them in the car. I'll go and fetch them," Mrs Hankinson said, getting up. "Must keep up the intussusception, eh?"

"Don't bother. You finish your tea. I can get them myself."

Joyce went out of the front door and walked over to the small blue car. The front and back seats were full of kleenex, cigar and cigarette packets, old torn maps, magazines, and, in the corner of the passenger seat, a plastic bag bulging with folded newspapers which had been picked up from the village post office four miles away. Joyce tucked them under her arm and returned to the house, spreading them out over the kitchen table.

"You're an amazing woman, Joyce," Mrs Hankinson said, lighting a cheroot. "I've never known anyone take such trouble to keep up with things. Me, I just get it off the radio — when the fucking thing isn't falling in the bath — or the telly. But to wade through that lot! What are you looking for all the time? Revelations?"

"This is a reading house," Joyce replied amiably "I should be with Malcolm in London today meeting some Danes but I thought better of it when he gave me a list of all he had to get through with them. There just wouldn't be enough opportunity to chat, if you know what I mean."

Mrs Hankinson pulled hard on her cheroot and blew a plume of smoke at the ceiling.

"What would you say to these Danes?" she asked, lowering her round, over-bright eyes. "You know that they're the number one pornographers? All the worst of that stuff comes from Denmark."

"I wouldn't avoid that subject if that's what they're famous for," Joyce murmured, her fingertips running over the newsprint. "Do you know the names of any famous people from Denmark?"

"Hamlet!" Mrs Hankinson said triumphantly. "He was a Dane."

"But he's from the imagination," Joyce replied, sitting down to a feature article on common land and rights of way in modern Britain. "I like to know about real people if I can and then get on to the fiction."

Mrs Hankinson opened a cupboard and rolled out a giant orange vacuum cleaner.

"Well, Joyce, I'll leave you to your studies. I've got work to do. You know, when Malcolm designed this place he should have thought about what it would be like to clean. It's an absolute bugger."

Mrs Hankinson trundled the vacuum cleaner out of the kitchen and into a lift to ascend to the east bedroom tower. Upon entering, her finger remained on the button in order to hold the door for Joyce who she knew would be following with her arms full of newspapers. Together they arose to Stagg's bedroom and Joyce spread her journals, tabloid and broadsheet, over the bed, chatting to Mrs Hankinson while the vacuum cleaner hummed, sometimes listening to the woman's harangues, sometimes reading out interesting sections from the articles and comment in the papers. In this manner, with variations between the daily help's emotional turmoils and the ratiocinative musings of the nation's editors, Joyce spent the morning until Mrs Hankinson left, having finished her work for the day.

Instead of making lunch for herself Joyce put on her coat and a pair of short red wellington boots and went for a walk along the shore, using the time to digest all she had heard and read that morning. A cold, steady wind blew from the north-east quarter —all the way from Siberia, as Malcolm never tired of telling her —and the tide was far out, the edge of the sea invisible in the reflected sunlight on the wet sands. She saw the gulls wheeling and diving in the abounding space; where they flew was the line of the creeping foam, the sea's lip. An urge to walk out to it was difficult to resist but she made the effort, knowing that it would be ill-advised to test her physical resources that far. From her years on the Dee estuary she knew all about the speed of the tide over sand where the sea went out a long way then returned with hungry swiftness, catching the idler unawares. Malcolm had spent a night on Little Hilbre that way, caught by the tide. Every time Joyce recalled the event, fear tightened her throat and her heart beat faster. It was not because death had been near; such trepidations fade, but that her son had been completely alone, cut off, isolated. Joyce had gone to the shore to look for him, guessing what had happened. She had been able to enlist the help of a fluke-fisher with a rubber-tyred cart. The man had driven his old horse far beyond safety, the water up to its chest, but just short of the island a raging gully had proved too deep. She remembered her son erect on the red rock of a promontory, the wind lifting his hair as he bawled bravely that he would sit out the tide and there was no need to worry. Joyce had sat up all night, then, at four in the morning, walked to the shore and waded out with the retreating tide, a shopping-bag with a thermos of hot tea and some sandwiches and a blanket in her hand. They had met each other half-way, the boy numb with cold, his eyes reddened with sleeplessness, and Joyce had stood there in the swirling water while he drank and fed, his body pressed against her under the blanket, the edges of which had trailed in the sea, causing her to tut and fuss while his major mischief went unreprimanded, so glad she had been to have him back all in one piece.

For a while she followed the ragged line of the tide's debris; wood, plastic bottles, a hair-comb from summer somewhere, mashed shells, weed and wrack, the scourings of the North Sea. When she looked up from the introverted depths into which these images of desuetude drew her, she saw the house in its true setting. Malcolm had told her that Hilbre was best approached from the sea. Now it was clear in its statement: an island with look-out towers, a defence which sucked in the outside and encouraged invasion, a balanced, poised place which was habitation and invitation.

Stagg's mother increased her pace as she stepped through the looser dry sand, stumbling in her need to regain the shelter of the open fort which her son had constructed on the fringe of her known world.

Malcolm Stagg got home late that night. He was tired after his trip and went straight up to bed. Within fifteen minutes he was undressed, washed and asleep, a half-moon beaming down upon him through the glass from a clear night sky.

If he had thought about his mother at this hour it would only have been to check that she was safe in the west bedroom tower, visible from his own. Any light that was on would have told him that Joyce was still awake and he might have picked up his bedside telephone to have a word with her before going to sleep. But the tower had been dark, its glass glittering in the moonlight. His assumption that his mother was asleep, comfortable, at ease in the world, secure in his house, was a reasonable one given his fatigue, but a closer look at the west tower would have shown a window open and a pale face framed, looking up at the moon then down at a large picture book about astronomy as Joyce plumbed the ancient problem of how the moon comes and goes in the heavens, and the immediate question of why now, at this time of her life, she found this motion so acutely upsetting.

Chapter Two

Next morning Stagg got up early and went into his extensive work-suite: office, draughting and computer rooms, kitchen and conveniences, and applied himself to a commission for the headquarters building of an Alsace winery. He heard the adjoining door being tried at nine o'clock and knew that it was his mother but he did not open it, or reply to the intercom when Joyce shouted, "I know you're in there!" through the system half an hour later.

When he had finished the task which he had allotted to himself for the day, he turned out all the lights, left the suite, and locked it behind him, leaving the telephone on an answering-machine. He had decided that the rest of his time that weekend would be spent on his mother.

He found her sitting in a shell-shaped armchair in the hall. It was one of those chairs in one of those places where people are never expected to sit and where the functions of the furniture and the space are uncertain.

"Ah, there you are," Stagg said, bending his neck in what amounted to a bow. "Have you had some lunch?"

"I feel very strange today, Malcolm," Joyce replied vacantly.

"And where shall we go this afternoon," Stagg enquired, guiding the exchange away from this inauspicious start. "You mentioned that you'd like to go to Walsingham to see the medieval shrine."

"Did I?"

"Yes," Stagg continued, anxious to get away from any discussion of strangeness. "You told me all about it: how the lady of the manor had a vision, then went to Jerusalem . . . "

Joyce held up a hand.

With a start Stagg saw a half-smoked cheroot held between her fingers.

"What are you smoking?" he demanded in surprise.

"Mrs Hankinson gave me one of hers. It's from Java," Joyce replied, shaking her head as if to clear it of fumes. "I must say, I can't get along with the tobacco."

Stagg leaned forward; with a disapproving tut he pulled the stub of the cheroot free from her fingers and dropped it into the tray of a boot-scraper beside the front door.

"You promised me that you'd stopped smoking," he said severely.

"I said I'd stopped smoking cigarettes," Joyce replied with a quick blue blaze of defiance in her eyes.

"It was reasonable for me to assume that that included cigars. Perhaps you've been smoking a pipe as well?"

Joyce struggled out of the chair and hung on to her son's arm, gesturing towards the door.

"Let's have some fresh air," she whispered. "My throat's gone musty."

The east wind smote them as they opened the door and stepped out. Stagg looked questioningly at his mother but she pushed him over the step and on to the gravel, pulling the door shut behind her.

"This will blow away the cobwebs," she said, taking his arm. "Did you see your fancy woman yesterday?"

Stagg faltered. It had been his intention to confess his lie about Denmark and East Germany within the next few minutes and he already had it scripted in his mind. Once that was over he planned to show his mother some passport application forms which he had picked up in Petty France, London, the day before. The promise of foreign travel would earn him full absolution even though it was to a place she had not expected to go at this time.

"Tell me about her," Joyce persisted, jerking his arm. "I don't like to think that you're doing without."

His plans in tatters, Stagg rounded the bull-nosed corner of the house and got into the lee of the wind.

"That's my private life, Ma," he said, his voice shaded with pleading. "I look after that myself."

"Don't call me Ma, call me Joyce," she replied with a grimace. "The age of Ma is over. We can talk about anything, you and me. What's her name? Rosamund?"

"Why Rosamund?" Stagg asked, sensing a chance of escape from the primary question. "Do you know someone called Rosamund?"

"I did once, at school. She told me that her name meant *rose of the world*." Joyce looked over the lawns to the huge fields of the nearby farms, green prairies of wheat. "I don't like to think of you being frustrated. It's not fair on a full-grown man."

Stagg blushed, his feelings performing acrobatics down in his belly. "I didn't meet any Danes, yesterday," he hastened to confess, "that was said to confuse you. With things as they are, my business is politically sensitive. Everyone assumes that I'm in the know about what makes post-communist countries tick, but I'm not. My clients only expect architecture for their money. They couldn't care less about my opinions." He stopped, aware that his mother was looking at him pityingly. "What's up?" he asked.

"You're so inhibited, son."

"I thought that if you knew that these clients were from East Germany and we were planning to build an opera house, you'd pump me with questions about what's going on there. Who cares what's going on in Denmark? I'm not a prophet, I don't have a crystal ball."

"What does Rosamund do for a living?"

"I didn't say her name was Rosamund."

"It's a working title. Confide in me. Give me the name of a famous person who came from East Germany."

"Handel, Bach . . . "

Joyce pulled a twig of flowering cherry close and slipped her fingers either side of the blossom like a button-stick.

"Musicians."

"Yes."

Joyce let the twig go, wiping moisture off her fingers.

"What we've all been through since the last war. Do you realise, son, that's all it's been about? The last war. Breaking free of it. Why do these East Germans want you for their opera house?"

"Don't ask me, ask them."

"I'd like to meet these people. I hated Germans for years. There're lots of questions I'd like to ask them. Can you arrange it?"

"Rosamund is a radiographer," Stagg interposed quickly.

"What is it they got wrong? When I look at state communism I can't see why it doesn't work, except that people don't really like being governed. There's nothing nice about it, is there? Why do we have to put up with it? When you're building this opera house I'll come over and talk to these characters."

Stagg took the passport application forms out of his inside pocket and put them into Joyce's hand.

"Fill these in as soon as you can," he said, carefully casual.

His mother stared at the envelope, then pulled a corner of a form out and studied the cryptic reference numbers printed there in heavy, black type.

"It's for a passport. You'll need your birth certificate," Stagg added after a long pause. "Don't you think its time that you stepped outside your native land?"

"I wish you wouldn't avoid big issues," his mother said with regret, a deep cleft of puzzlement between her eyes. "Why do you do that? All I was going to say was that it's not natural for a man of your age to be without sex." She held the envelope up so that it fluttered in the breeze which was swooping round the corner, spillage from a shore-wind. "I think it's cruel. It could drive a person mad."

"Yes, Joyce," Stagg responded, his voice low. "But forget it."

"I never took a vow of chastity. It was just how it worked out."

He made no reply, not wanting to go down that track any further.

Joyce flared her fine nostrils, folding the envelope in half then in half again. As her fingers bent the forms for the third time Stagg wondered if she was trying to break some kind of record.

"It's cruel, I blame it for a lot. It was the only way that women could practice birth-control, being cruel. It caused a lot of rows in our house. My view is that there hasn't been a world war since the last one because the Pill came along and took the sting out of married life. The

23

men no longer want to kill each other on such a big scale." She finished her point, the envelope now a small U-shaped nodule in the palm of her hand. "You never did National Service, did you?"

Stagg shook his head and said that he had been very glad to be spared that particular waste of time.

"All we thought about was the cruelty when they were at home, and the cruelty when they were away at the war. My mother felt very sorry for the men. They had the worst of it, she always said. She was a good woman in many ways. I miss her very much. If I could talk to her now about . . . " She hesitated, looking up as if she expected to see her mother flying past. " . . . Well, the Virgin Mary, for instance, I wouldn't need books, would I?"

Stagg concurred, steering a course which would take them back to the security of Hilbre's interior, a setting which made dealing with Joyce easier, somehow. Here in the open air she had nothing to cage her, her mind bumping along like an inflatable raft in a sea of broken ice.

"Has Rosamund always wanted to be a radiographer?" she asked. "It's not much of a job is it, taking X-rays? One chest is much like another, I'd have thought. What does she think when she sees yours? Has that ever crossed your mind?"

"No, it hasn't."

"It would be the first thing I'd think about. What people do and how they treat each other is closely connected. Your great-grandfather on my father's side was a grave-digger at Fazakerly. He buried his own wife and two daughters." She paused and winked. "So, we're off to Berlin?"

Stagg surrendered and laughed out loud. This release was a cue for Joyce to start unfolding the passport forms which she did with the care of a seamstress.

"I didn't say it was Berlin. They're not ready for you yet."

"Well, some day, perhaps? I've got it on my list. So where are we going?"

He freed his arm and put it round her shoulders. "I'll tell you when the time is right," he said. "Until then let's leave it as a surprise."

★

24

Stagg drove his mother to Walsingham that afternoon. He had a cassette of the twelfth-century *Jeu de Daniel* from Beauvais, which he played to help her get into the right mood. After a minute of the reverberatory old instruments and elongated tempi Joyce told him to turn it off because it was disturbing her contemplation.

"What are you thinking about?" Stagg asked respectfully.

"I'm preparing my brain for this visit."

"Walsingham's another ten miles now," he said, adjusting his seat and hunching his shoulders. "Not long."

"I've never been out of this country, you know. That says a lot about me, I think. Couldn't be bothered to travel. It's shameful when you think about this Norman woman nine hundred years ago who walked from here to Jerusalem."

"I'm not sure that she walked," Stagg said with a brief, sideways look to check if Joyce was genuinely upset. She had often been in tears during the last six months. The relentless activity of her mind had sometimes driven her to weep with vexation, wishing that it would give her some rest. But she was dry-eyed, peering at a notebook in which she was writing with a large pink ball-point pen.

"What are you writing?" he asked.

"None of your business, but if you must know it's about Robert Graves."

"Why him?"

"I read that book of his, *The White Something.*"

"All of it?" Stagg said with chuckle.

"Yes, it took me till half-past four this morning. Did you find it confusing?"

Stagg admitted that he had never read *The White Goddess* all the way through but had dipped into it many years ago while married to Vanessa, his first wife.

"She was into the earth-mother thing," he said with a snort. "To me it was phoney nonsense. To be honest, I didn't believe a word of it."

"Vanessa was certainly no earth mother," Joyce agreed, closing her notebook and putting the top on her pen with a hollow, plastic clunk which was derogatory. "But she was intelligent. In some ways

I'd say she was more intelligent than you, Malcolm, but she had no soul to speak of."

Stagg was silent. Whenever he remembered the final years with Vanessa, his tongue cleaved to the roof of his mouth. They had been terrible, ferocious times which had brought him to the edge of despair.

"Would you mind if I listened to the music?" he asked suddenly, his hand already reaching out for the button. "It will do something for me even if it can't get through to you."

"You go ahead, son, don't mind me. I know you think about her. You think about them all. I suppose you must dream about them too. That must be the worst."

Stagg maintained his silence, his fingers wrapped a little tighter round the rim of the steering-wheel.

"Do you dream about them?" she persisted.

He grunted his reply, unwilling to extract the sourness from it. Yes, Stagg did dream about them, so what?

"What do you dream?"

Out of the corner of his eyes Stagg saw the notebook come out of her hand-bag and he heard the clunk of the pink ball-point pen being prepared for action.

"I can't remember," he said stiffly.

"Is it physical?"

"D'you mean, do we knock each other around?" he responded jokily, but with an unambiguous undercurrent of meaning which said: 'Leave this topic, please!'

"I've been a widow since 1943. No man has ever taken your father's place. Since his last leave I haven't had any sex with anyone, but I don't dream about it. After reading that book last night I have to say I'm surprised." Her finger shot out and stabbed at the reject button on the cassette-player. "Do you ever dream about having sex with me?"

The car swerved and touched the grass verge as Stagg reacted to his mother's question. A weathered sign announced that Walsingham was only three miles away. In a voice which was as strained and convoluted as a conch, Stagg remarked to his mother that they were nearly there.

26

"I know that you must have done. All males do, so I'm told," Joyce went on. "But I don't fully understand it. Do you?"

Stagg stretched the corners of his mouth into what passed for a grimace of consenting ignorance.

"Some of these theories aren't much use." She sighed and underlined a phrase in her notebook. "I was doing my speed-reading in top gear last night and I've garbled quite a bit of what I wrote down, but there's one here I'd like your opinion on. 'Motherhood', it says, 'is a power which is so deeply organic that it is unknowable.' Now, I'll be straight with you, Malcolm, I can't remember whether I wrote that or Robert Graves came up with it."

Stagg seized his chance to shift his mother's attention from the particular — where he was pinned out like a guinea-pig with its belly slit open — to the general where the substantial figure of Mr Graves was recumbent in eternity, unconcerned and intact.

"It sounds like Graves," Stagg muttered. "A typical cop-out."

"Why a cop-out?"

"It's all guesswork. Just because we can't fully analyse a phenomenon we say it's unknowable. When you look at what he's saying it's specious. We can understand the organic. We can break it down. Nothing is unknowable. What a claim to make in this day and age! If Robert Graves was here right now I'd laugh in his face."

With a savage twist of the steering-wheel Stagg turned his car into the roadside and parked by the Slipper Chapel where pilgrims once left their shoes before completing the last stretch to the shrine of Our Lady of Walsingham barefoot.

Stagg was a thorough person. Once he had his mother in the tourist trap of the village, he insisted that every feature of it be visited. Joyce's enthusiasm was limited once she discovered that Richeldis de Faverches, the lady of the manor in the legend, had not actually gone to Jerusalem on foot at all, but had only seen a vision of the Virgin telling her to build a copy of the house in Nazareth where Jesus had been brought up. Joyce was scathing that her son, a successful architect, had never asked himself where the plans had come from.

"I'm not impressed," Joyce grumbled as they waited to be served in a cafeteria. "This is all superstition, Malcolm. What is it to do with life today?"

"You don't find it interesting that people spent so much time and energy following up this myth?" Stagg said moodily, his long fingers playing with the edge of the red check tablecloth. "I would have thought that it would be right up your street."

"You don't understand," Joyce countered. "Anyone can say they've had a vision but not many people could walk to Jerusalem."

A fraught waitress delivered a pot of tea and two slices of Battenberg cake. Joyce did not halt the flow of her open meditation as the girl unloaded her tray.

"All this is wishful thinking, from what I can see. When Henry the Eighth wrecked the shrine and chopped the head off the prior or whoever he was, they should have left it at that. All this bring-back-the-church stuff in central Europe worries me. Did they suffer for nothing? Can't we have a world without fucking superstition for once?"

The waitress stood by the table, the tray hanging from her hand, her mouth open. Joyce looked up.

"What's the matter with you?" she said haughtily.

Stagg covered his eyes with his hand as the girl retreated, affronted and upset.

"Why have you suddenly started swearing?" Stagg hissed.

Joyce straightened her back and took hold of the teapot in a firm grip. "You're not ready for the future, Malcolm," she chided him with a toss of her head, her hand steady as she poured the tea. "When it comes down to it you're a stick-in-the-mud. All your education did was to fill you with history."

Stagg stirred his tea then cut his slice of Battenberg cake into four quarters, two yellow and two pink. As he tinkered with this piece of geometry he sourly advised his mother against believing that bad language was an oral badge of enlightenment.

"All you're concerned with is huts," Joyce came back at him. "What do you know, son? Greek huts, Roman huts, Gothic huts. Son, I haven't got the time to get bogged down. I have to go straight to the heart. Mrs Hankinson used the eff-word to me this morning when she was telling me about dropping the radio in the bath. She said . . . "

"I don't want to know what she said, thank you," Stagg replied, "and I'm going to give her the sack."

Stagg's mother did not speak to him for the rest of the day. After a tense drive back from Walsingham, she went up to her room and stayed there, refusing to come down and share the table with him at dinner. When he went up to bed that night he saw all the lights blazing in the western tower and heard the sound of loud music. He rang her several times but she had left the receiver off the hook. His purpose in wanting to speak to her had not been either to apologise or withdraw his decision to terminate Mrs Hankinson's employment, but merely to lead his mother into safer pastures. Much as he loved her, and had always been amused by her idiosyncracies, he was beginning to be alarmed. When he put himself in her place and guessed at the turbulence which had projected her into her new mental state he could not help but be anxious. For fifty years she had lived a simple working life, too simple, and too scornful of the greater world, if truth be told. She had been at pains to be independent, very proud of her strength. What concessions she had made to his wealth had been strictly limited; an annual holiday, short visits, but no income, no stream of gifts, no easing of the financial rigours within which she had always operated. In fact she had attempted to give *him* money, unable to get out of the habit of slipping him five pound notes whenever he seemed crestfallen.

This was a strict code of conduct for her: it included a robust disapproval of all his tastes in music, art, literature as well as many of his friends, which could be softened by reason but would always flare up at the slightest provocation. Anything which had cast doubts upon the validity of her life by comparison with his had been resolutely attacked and vanquished. Stagg had never fought these battles, preferring to be passive in case she should decide to shut him out. In his own mind he argued that for a woman who had started work at fourteen, having no education beyond basic literacy and numeracy, been married at twenty-one, widowed at twenty-three, spent the next six months in a munitions factory with the unborn, fatherless Stagg in her womb, then laboured twenty years for his good, she had a resilience worth preserving. Whatever concessions she made to him as the weakness of age approached he would see to it that her pride would never be dented. This resolution had never left him, even during this unsettling period when he had sometimes wondered about her sanity.

He was wakened by the bedside telephone ringing. As he answered it he glanced at the luminous numbers on his clock. It was ten past three.

"Is that you, son?" she said.

"It is."

"Are you alone?"

"I am."

"You can speak then?"

"I can. What's on your mind?"

He could see the lights shining from the western tower but the music had ceased. Out in the fields behind the house he heard the bark of a fox.

"It's my fault," Joyce said down the telephone. "I've let Mrs Hankinson get too close. I've been a cleaning-woman myself, you remember."

Stagg paused, realising that once he associated himself with this memory he would be forced to agree that Mrs Hankinson should be kept on.

"Were you?" he replied, doing his best to keep the equivocation out of his voice.

"You should be able to remember. You used to carry the bucket. Those were the days."

He heard the click as she put the receiver down. He laid his head on the pillow, taking his defeat as calmly as he could.

Chapter Three

Three weeks later Stagg and his mother flew to Tunis and from thence journeyed south to the coastal town of Sousse. Mrs Hankinson, temporarily estranged from her husband, was left to house-sit. Joyce treated her first ascent in an aeroplane with seriousness, saying that any fear of flying would make her participation in the real space age difficult, so it must be conquered. She went to the toilet four times during the two-hour flight, and engaged the man next to her in a conversation about the Roman hypocaust.

"It's like the under-floor heating I had in my flat," Stagg heard her say, "but they used steam. These cities in Tunisia are enormous. My husband is buried between two of them up in the mountains. My son always promised to take me there and now we're going. What I'll feel I don't know, love. So long it's been. The War Graves Commission sent me a photograph of the grave, then they dug him up off the battlefield and buried him somewhere else, then they dug him up again and finally let him rest. I have photographs of each grave. The first marker just gave his name and rank. The second had the serial number as well, but these were both shared between the six of them — they all got blown up together — then the third was his own, with an epitaph which I chose out of a book which they sent me. When I chose it I knew what I meant but now I'm not so sure."

The man, a genial young father from Bedford who was taking his wife and daughters on holiday, asked Joyce what the epitaph was. She took out her notebook.

"D'you know, son, I can't ever remember it properly. Where are we?" She flicked through the first pages, running her finger up and down the lines. "I wrote it in my book so I could work everything out before we went up into the mountains to find the cemetery. Here we are!" With the notebook laid out on her lap she looked at Stagg. "You listen to this as well, Malcolm. It concerns you."

Stagg smiled apologetically at the young father, sending him a telepathic message of sympathy for getting involved.

"God proved him and found him worthy of himself." Joyce flipped the notebook shut. "What's that all about? Why did I choose it? It could mean so many things. I must have been confused. What do you think it means, son?"

Stagg and the man from Bedford looked at each other, uncertain who was being addressed.

"Any ideas? I can't find it in the Bible. Perhaps the War Office paid someone to make these epitaphs up by the yard? Even so, I'm intrigued. 'God proved him and found him worthy of himself.' Malcolm, you answer me this question: worthy of God, or himself?"

"I don't think it's existentialist," Stagg said. "Epitaphs are usually God-orientated. Has *himself* got a capital letter?"

"Do you understand that?" Joyce asked the man from Bedford.

"I'm sure he's right," he replied cheerfully, "but I'm only a person who runs a garden centre."

"Then you're blessed," Joyce said, putting her notebook away, "but I'll tell you this much. The idea that someone is worthy of themself is much more interesting than whether she's worthy of God. We don't know God from Adam."

The man from Bedford made a noise through his nose and pulled the ring on a can of beer to cover his bafflement.

"I don't care what time of night we get to our hotel," he said, crushing the can after he had emptied it into a plastic glass. "I'm going for a swim in the sea. I've never been as bored as I have this last winter. When I looked around all I could see was mess. So little happens, you see. Nothing grows much. The difference between January and June is fantastic."

A woman in the seat in front got up, opened the overhead compartment and took out a small white pillow and a red blanket. Joyce copied her, watching to see what the woman did next through the gap between the seats. When she had placed the pillow behind her head and covered herself with the blanket, she burst out laughing.

"I haven't had a swim since 1942," she said.

"Why's that?" the man from Bedford asked, his eyebrows raised in genuine surprise. "It's great, swimming. My favourite sport."

"She thought she might drown herself," Stagg found himself saying for his mother, having heard the story before.

The man from Bedford thrust his lower lip forward and cradled the glass of beer in the crutch of his jeans. He made no further comment, signalling to Stagg and his mother that he needed time to be with his own thoughts and the conversation came to an end.

Below them the scratched pewter of the sea changed into the black of Africa.

Joyce liked the hotel. It was a white, airy building, tiled in golden brown, surrounded by flowering trees and palms, busy with servants in starched uniforms and tall, tasselled fezzes. The dining-room was vast and quiet with hundreds of individual tables laid out in an indecipherable design that reflected the twists and turns of the serpentine plasterwork which writhed over the ceiling. Joyce felt that nothing had weight in this place, there was no substance. Each hour was a delightfully inconsequential period between meals and walks along the beach; and each day was a dream before the looming reality of the drive into the mountains. She knew that Stagg felt the same; he showed his light-headedness in his own way, being gentler than usual, drifting through conversations with his mother like a man in a punt, a navigator along the shaded stream of indolence who can hear the distant waterfall. He saw how brave she was, and how simple still, in spite of all her questing.

On the evening of the fourth day he went for a nocturnal walk along the shore after his mother had gone to bed. He made a decision to go right round the shallow bay, trotting and walking alternately, his bare feet splashing through the shallows. A quarter of a mile from the hotel he came upon the first landmark, a concrete pillbox sunk at a tilt in the sand. As he trotted past it a youth came out of the moon-shadow and accosted him.

Stagg ran faster, his eyes fixed on the phosphorescent sea.

"What's the matter? Can't you say no?" the youth yelled after him, setting off in pursuit, joined by two colleagues who scrambled out of the pillbox.

Stagg did not increase his pace. He was determined to keep his dignity and, as a man of meaty middle age, he knew that he could never outrun them. When they caught up with him they pranced along in a line on his heels, dark circus horses neighing obscenities and prices. Eventually he could stand it no longer: with his feet planted in the underwater sand he defied them.

"Old ruin!" One youth shouted, kicking water up. "Go to bed!"

The other two aped the first, cavorting, screaming, drenching him. There was nothing to do but wait for them to stop. When they tired of the fun they spat at him, snarled in Arabic, then hared off back towards the pillbox, having heard a summoning whistle.

Stagg left the shore and crossed the garden of another hotel to reach a road which ran parallel to the coast back to where he was staying. He was barefoot and the loose stone on the surface pricked his soles. Within a hundred yards of the point where he had joined the road, he was accosted again from behind a set of gates, then from a group of palms. By the time that he reached the security of his hotel he felt that the country where his father lay buried was haunted by the harlotry which had followed all armies since man first raised his hand against his neighbour.

The dream had gone and it was time to go into the wilderness.

He had breakfast early, remaining at the table with a book until his mother appeared. As soon as she entered the dining-room he could see that she was not well.

"I didn't sleep a wink," she said as she sat down.

"Nor did I."

"Something has disagreed with me. I think the food is too greasy. Do you find that when you don't feel so good you can't think straight?"

He had been ready to go to the hotel desk and hire a car for the day, having worked out that he should be able to drive to the cemetery and back before it got too late; but this plan obviously had to be put aside in view of her frailty.

"I had dreams, things running through my mind. Why do I need so little sleep these days? I've forgotten what a good night's sleep is like, waking up feeling rested. It's an ordeal, isn't it, son?"

He watched her drink tea and eat bread, marvelling at her coolness. All night he had tossed and turned, the enormity of what he had done by bringing her to this corrupted sepulchre, tormenting him. For fifty years it had been a photograph. Now it was all around her in its ugliness and there was worse to come, no doubt.

"Are you glad you came?" he blurted out.

"Oh, yes!"

"You could have said no if you'd wanted."

"Of course I could."

She consumed another piece of bread and pushed a stray lock of hair back under her headband.

"Are you having second thoughts, Malcolm?"

"Not if you're all right. It's been left so long, this trip. We all change. When I first asked you if you'd like to come you were quite different about many things. To be frank, I don't think you were all that interested."

"I wasn't," she agreed. "I had a job in an office. There wasn't any hurry to do anything exciting. If I'd gone then I'd never have been able to go back to work and sit there watching the clock. Something would have had to be done about *me*."

Joyce gulped at her tea to mask her sudden, powerful feelings, hoping that her son would not notice, but he had immediately picked up her distress signal.

"That was very sensible, working it out like that," he said softly. "We'll have a better time leaving it till now."

"I'm a lot tougher, for a start," Joyce sniffed, using her napkin to wipe her eyes. "And I know more about myself. That's been useful, I can tell you. In those days when I was working in John Lewis there wasn't a thing I had to say for myself. I lived through you, which is a crime. No one has the right to double up someone else's burden."

Stagg ran his finger down the spine of his book.

"We'll go tomorrow," he said, his heart lighter now. "I'll order a packed lunch off the waiter."

"I didn't mean what I said just now," Joyce said. "I never lived through you at all."

"Oh," Stagg murmured, unsure about the morality of his disappointment. "Not a good idea in most cases."

"I had my own system, you see, a job I could do standing on my head, a routine, a place to live, and I made it work."

"Yes," Stagg said heartily, "you did."

"But I could only keep it going if I didn't let my imagination loose. The imagination can be a curse."

"Yes."

"You say yes, Malcolm, but the question is: why are we half-dead when we're forty and fully alive when we're all washed up?" She briskly dunked a corner of her bread into her tea then dipped it into the sugar bowl.

"Shall we go up into the mountains tomorrow?" Stagg asked, his eyes fixed on the brown lumps left behind on the slopes of the white dunes of sugar. "The weather forecast is good."

"Have I wasted my life?"

"No, of course not."

"What am I doing here?" She looked around the vast room as if it were a prison cell. "Is this your idea of a holiday?"

"Do you want to put it off for a few days?"

Joyce got up, threw her napkin on to the table and walked the length of the dining-room with her head held high. From the freshly watered garden came an aura of warm, mixed light, bathing one side of her body. Stagg picked up her handbag and followed her, his heart beating with anxiety.

She was afraid.

★

36

He left it for three days before bringing the subject up again. Joyce had made excuses not to leave the hotel, remaining either in her room or the grounds, and she had missed meals or had them alone, deliberately waiting until Stagg had finished before going to the table. When they did meet up she was taciturn and evasive, refusing to talk about anything but the most trivial matters. As he watched her struggling with herself, Stagg realised that she was attempting to reoccupy her old life. She was using the hotel as her flat, pretending that the corridors were the streets she had walked along to work when she had been in control. The notebook did not make an appearance, but the tabloid British newspapers available at the desk were always under her arm.

He waylaid her at dinner on the third day, watching the door to her room from a seat in the garden. She had left it until the last minute, hoping to avoid him. When he followed her into the dining-room and pulled her chair out with exaggerated politeness, she exclaimed crossly: "I don't like being spied on!"

Stagg made no apology. He ordered his food from the menu and scanned the wine-list.

"You've been drinking," Joyce complained. "I don't want to sit and have my dinner with a drunk."

Stagg ordered a Haut Médoc, folded his hands, put them on the table, cocked his head to one side and smiled toothily.

"What have you been up to, then?" he said.

"Nothing," came the curt answer.

"I've been for three swims in the sea, two walks along the beach, a visit to a carpet shop . . ."

"Don't you be smart with me, Malcolm Stagg!"

"And I've had thoughts. Want to hear them? Are you thinking much?" Stagg chattered on, his tone edged with satire which he recognised as unpleasant, but he could not hold himself back. Weakness did this to him, sometimes. If indulged it aroused hostility which was dangerous, especially when alcohol was in his blood. "How long shall we stay here? A few years?"

"Now you're showing your true colours," Joyce said, her face grey with shame. "Can't you afford a little understanding?"

She had chosen the right riposte. Stagg's surge of aggression and impatience abated. As the waiter delivered the wine, a white cloth swathing the long neck of the bottle, Stagg hid behind the man's flourishes, his grin of apology ridiculously boyish.

"You'll like this wine," he promised.

"Haven't you had enough?" Joyce said bitterly; then, with venom: "Why can't you give me some time? It's been fifty years, for God's sake!"

"All right, all right," Stagg sighed, "no one's rushing you. My father won't run away, will he?" He drank from his wine. "Mmm. Not bad."

Joyce's lower jaw dropped in astonishment. A frown cleaved her forehead, driving her straight eyebrows down together in an arrow's point. Her eyes seemed to inflate into a bursting, blue stare.

"What did you say?" she demanded.

"I said the wine's not bad," Stagg replied with an air of innocence. "Try it."

Joyce took a pause, put her fingers around the stem of her glass then threw the contents into his face. As the other diners turned to watch the scene, interpreting it as a lovers' tiff between bizarre paramours, she got hold of the bottle and emptied it into his lap.

The hotel manager, an old Frenchman, asked them to leave, refunding the whole amount which had been paid in advance and, in order to facilitate the removal, arranged alternative accommodation at an hotel run by his brother at the other end of the settlement. The transfer was made on the same night as the fracas itself, Stagg and his mother being whisked away in a transit van which was covered in dust from a desert journey. Joyce sat on a bench-seat sandwiched between a stack of laundered sheets and a carton of fly-spray, her eyes fixed on the back of her son's head as the van was driven along the palm-lined avenue, over waste ground, up a low hill, coming to a halt in front of an unfinished development which had diggers and cranes standing idle at one end while attempts to landscape a new garden had been made at the other.

"I'm not staying here," Joyce announced.

"It's only for one night," Stagg said wearily. "Tomorrow we'll decide what to do."

"I'm not staying in somewhere that's not finished. That's the last thing I want at the moment."

The driver had already taken out the cases and dropped them at the entrance to the unlit foyer. Before Stagg could argue with him, the man got back in the van and drove off.

"Well, it looks as though we haven't really got a choice," Stagg said with a harsh laugh, pushing at the door which did not give way.

"And you just accepted it," Joyce came back at him. "Why didn't you tell that hotel manager where to get off? People are entitled to have arguments, aren't they? What's so sacred about his dining-room? Shall I tell you what I think? It's because I'm a woman. If you'd attacked me that would have been all right."

Stagg sighed, making sure that his mother heard the note of exhaustion in his voice. The door would not budge and there was no sign of a bell in the wall of plate glass which was the hotel entrance. Walking backwards he looked over the façade of the building, noting where lights shone. They appeared to be corridor illuminations.

"I don't think anyone's at home," he said finally.

"Good."

"Any bright ideas as to where we're going to sleep?"

"I don't care. You can stick me in the cement-mixer if you like."

Stagg sat down on his suitcase. Joyce wandered into the starlight, taking a packet of cigarettes out of her handbag and lighting up.

"D'you want one?" she asked. "They're local."

"No, thanks," Stagg replied gloomily, too tired to comment upon her regression into nerve-saving nicotine. He stood up, went to the plate glass doors and knocked with his knuckles. After a few moments he switched to the flats of his hands, pounding at the glass and kicking.

All his efforts produced no response. The foyer remained dark, the cranes stayed framed in the firmament, Joyce puffed at her cigarette.

"I wonder you didn't break that," she mused. "It looks as though we'll have to find somewhere else."

Stagg walked up and down, pondering. He could not expect his mother to carry heavy luggage back to other hotels, nor could he leave her or the luggage behind, recalling the youths who had baited him on the beach. There was no sign of life in the vicinity, no nearby houses, only the sound of the sea.

He looked at his watch. The luminous fingers were at ten past one.

"We'll have to sleep out," he declared flatly. "D'you mind?"

Chapter Four

Stagg ferried the luggage down through the half-made garden to the beach and found a sheltered spot beneath a wall which was overhung by mimosa bushes. While Joyce sat on the wall, Stagg opened his suitcase and took out two sweaters.

"Here, put this on," he told his mother, throwing one up to her. "It will get cold later on."

"Why don't we try to walk along the beach?" Joyce grumbled, struggling to get into the sweater.

"It's too far to carry all the luggage."

"We can bury it in the sand and come back for it in the morning."

"Imagine the state it would be in," Stagg replied firmly. "Besides, it's too late. If I'm going to have a row with that hotel manager I want to do it in broad daylight, in front of everyone."

Joyce got down off the wall and sat on the raincoat which Stagg had spread out for them to sit on. There was a land breeze which the mimosa bush protected them from, and the sea was calm. Overhead the night sky was thickly strewn with stars and a gibbous moon beamed down, enabling them to see each other clearly.

"We're not going to get much sleep," Joyce said without rancour. "I don't mind but you've had a busy day, son. Close your eyes."

Stagg shook his head and leant back against the wall.

"No, I'll keep watch. There are some odd people lurking about in this area at night."

Further down the beach he could see the pillbox standing drunkenly in the sand, a malevolent, humped sentinel. He strained his ears to listen for voices.

"The last time I went camping was in North Wales with the Aintree Cycling Club," Joyce said loudly. "I was eighteen."

"Hush!" Stagg hissed.

"Why?"

"I thought I heard something."

"You heard me telling you about going to North Wales, I hope. I was speaking, Malcolm, and I don't like being told to shut up."

Stagg closed his eyes and slid further down the wall, tucking a folded towel behind his head.

"Sorry, Joyce. I'm a bit nervous," he murmured.

She patted his hand lightly and spoke soothingly: "That's right, son. You go to sleep." After a moment she began to hum, then sing under her breath. Stagg recognised a lullaby from his childhood:

> "Singing lulla-lulla-lulla-lulla bye-byes,
> Do you want the moon to play with
> Or the stars to run away with,
> Then close your pretty eyes . . . "

Then he heard the sound of a match being struck.

"Please don't smoke, Joyce," he whispered tiredly.

"Why not?"

"People will see where we are."

"What people? There's no one here."

There was a pause. Joyce looked at her son, expecting an answer but he had fallen asleep, his head fallen forward on to his chest. She carefully opened her suitcase and took out a big beach-towel, covering him with it, then settled down with her back against the wall, looking beyond the moonlit beach to the sea. Three cigarettes later, she saw a shooting star and it excited her; getting to her feet she walked down to the water's edge then strolled through the shallows, her eyes on the heavens in case another star fell. When she reached the pillbox she looked at it uncomprehendingly, having noticed it for the first time. Sunk as it was in the sand, a huge lump of random matter, it could have been a meteor which had fallen from space.

The cigarettes were in her hand. She lit her fourth while crouching against the sloped wall. There was a strange smell of animals from the interior of the pillbox so she moved away, back to the swollen silver of the sea. No force on earth could frighten her now, she decided. Wherever it was that she had to go, she would do so bravely.

Stagg awoke with the sun in his eyes. He was painfully stiff and there was a crick in his neck. Joyce was not beside him, only the sandy suitcases. With a cry of concern he pulled himself erect and lumbered out on to the open sand. Further down the beach he saw two camels tethered by the pillbox. He ran down and found Joyce squatting in the sand with a diminutive, wrinkled Arab in a striped burnous who was smoking one of her cigarettes.

"This is my son Malcolm." Joyce said by way of introduction, "and this is Ahmed."

"Hello, Ahmed." Stagg held out his hand and grinned as a thin, dark arm crept out of the folds of the burnous and gave him a firm handclasp. "Lovely morning."

"*Bonjour*," Ahmed said, exposing a few yellow stubs of teeth. "*Vôtre maman est charmant.*"

"That means I'm charming, doesn't it?" Joyce smiled and fiddled with a scarf she was wearing tied round her head. "He remembers the war. He was here, on this very spot when the Germans were driven out of Africa. These camels were both babies."

"Does he speak English?" Stagg asked. "You seem to have covered a lot of ground."

"No, people like Ahmed and me don't need to talk each other's language. We know what we're saying."

Stagg looked at his watch. It was seven-twenty.

"Well, as you've made friends with Ahmed, perhaps you can stay with him while I walk down to the hotel and sort that bastard manager out? I'll come back for you in a taxi," he declared manfully, brushing sand off his trousers. "It shouldn't take long."

"That's all been looked after," Joyce replied. "We were only waiting for you to wake up before setting off."

43

An hour later Stagg and his mother entered the gates of the hotel astride Ahmed's camels, their luggage hanging around the necks of the tall, supercilious beasts. Ahmed led them up to the marble steps of the foyer and halted his animals in the centre of a ceramic pattern representing the zodiac.

The waiters in the dining-room abandoned the serving of breakfast and rushed out to the foyer steps in order to witness the confrontation as the French manager came out to face the mounted English. Stagg and his mother had the unkempt, roguish air of desert brigands, a style which they had worked on during the journey from their overnight camp on the beach.

At first the manager attempted to laugh it off, requesting that the cameleers should accompany him to his office to discuss the matter once the gist of the grievance had been barked out in robust French by Stagg. But this was refused. What was the point of getting his mother down from the camel — a difficult procedure, and dangerous — if the hotel company was not willing to admit liability for the wrongs it had done, for its lies, its indifference to the safety of its clients? The camels would be spurred to the nearest gendarmerie to report that a woman, well advanced in years, of delicate constitution, had been made to sleep out on the beach all night.

The manager looked around him. All the guests were streaming out of the dining-room to see what was happening. As Stagg continued to boom out accusations of incompetence, stupidity, cruelty and insensitivity from the back of the camel, Joyce's mount decided to empty its bowels over Aquarius, the water-carrier.

The manager had been in the hotel business for thirty years and seen fortunes made and lost. There were, he knew, certain types of guest who, once aggrieved, would not rest until his life had been made a misery. This tall, slightly stooped Englishman with his large brown eyes and jug-handle ears, had the stamp of this breed. Another factor which led the manager to suspect that he had a tough opponent was the fierce loudness of Stagg's voice, which sounded like the belling of branch-horned beasts when the blood is up.

Inwardly cursing his fate, the manager strode forward and

offered Joyce his hand to descend, his polished black shoes paddling through rivulets of camel urine.

"Welcome back, madame," he said courteously. "From now on you will be our special guest."

After dinner that night Stagg had a drink with the manager in his office and it was agreed that a move to a hotel in Tunis would be a better solution on both sides. In addition Stagg insisted upon a letter of apology and the use of the manager's telephone to make a reservation, also a taxi to go to the new hotel. This was accepted and the following morning saw Stagg and his mother leaving the hotel in a black Citroën saloon accompanied by two silent men in dark suits.

"Why have we got two drivers?" Joyce asked as the car left the gates and went down the avenue of palms. Stagg asked the men in the front seat the question in French, to which they replied in English.

"He is my brother," the driver said.

Joyce was quiet for a while, her eyes on the succession of hotels and gardens; then she returned to her enquiries.

"Why don't you have a sign on your car?"

"A sign of what?" the driver asked.

"A sign saying 'taxi'."

"In Tunisia we don't have this."

"Yes, you do. I've seen them," Joyce insisted.

"No, our kind of taxi does not have a sign. This is a top quality firm."

Joyce shrugged. When she offered the men cigarettes they examined the packet first and, once they had ascertained that the product was local, politely refused.

"We're going up to Madjez-el-Bab tomorrow," Joyce said conversationally. "Have you ever been? Perhaps these lads could drive us, Malcolm, and save you all the bother of hiring a car. How much would that cost?"

The driver looked at his brother and grinned.

"Too expensive," he said.

"And we want to go to a place called Dougga," Joyce told them. "It's an old Roman city. We're planning to go there once we've been to the cemetery."

The driver glanced over his shoulder, his face suddenly serious.

"Why are you going to the cemetery?"

"To see my father's grave," Stagg replied. "He was killed at the Battle of Long Stop Hill in 1943."

The driver stopped the car at a roadside café and turned to lean over the seat.

"And who is this dead soldier to you, madam?" he asked Joyce.

"My husband," Joyce replied with asperity, "and this here's my son. He's brought me before I die. I hope you'd do as much for your mother."

The men got out of the car without another word and went into the café. Stagg watched them sit at a table with small cups of coffee and begin an earnest discussion. Twenty minutes later they were still there, now more agitated with each other, waving their arms in the air and arguing.

"I'm going to find out what's going on," Stagg said, pulling the doorhandle to get out. It did not open. He tried the other one, leaning across his mother. That was locked too.

"Who the hell do they think they are?" he exploded, scrambling over to the front seat. Both doors were locked. He pounded on the horn button but it did not work without the ignition. The car had a sunroof which he tried to open, only to find it secure. Left with no other means of attracting the attention of the men in the café he banged on the window. The sound it made was dull and heavy, not carrying the distance.

"Don't worry, Ma," he puffed, clambering back over beside her, "I'll get to the bottom of this."

"I said it wasn't a taxi," Joyce said smugly.

Ten minutes later the men came to the car and let them out, fending off Stagg's release of pent-up fury by putting on a dumbshow of understanding and pained apology until he had expended all his rage and gone quiet. Then they gingerly touched

46

his quivering shoulders, said that they were sorry for the delay, and escorted Stagg and his mother across a dusty forecourt and into the café which was a makeshift affair with a few rusty metal chairs and tables under a trellis of convolvulus abutting a kitchen shed. Once they had all sat down the driver ordered coffee and small cakes.

"These are Tunisian specialities," he said. "This woman makes them herself."

"Never mind the cakes," Stagg retorted. "Tell us what's going on. You have no right to stop for a tea-break without asking our permission, and you certainly have no right to keep us locked in your car."

"We have plenty of rights," the driver replied, taking out a small wallet and showing Stagg an identity card. "We are immigration officers."

Stagg's jaw wobbled. He looked at Joyce whose expression was showing mild disconcertment but no real alarm.

"It's that manager," she said knowingly, "I never trusted him."

"What's all this about?" Stagg demanded. "Have you arrested us?"

The driver solemnly stirred his coffee.

"No," he said, "we're deporting you."

Stagg put his head in his hands, shaking it violently. He felt the urge to lift the table up over his head and hurl it into a nearby field of sunflowers. Caution was at work in his mind, however, and he kept his anger at bay.

"What is our crime?" he asked quietly, gripping his knees hard in the effort to hold his voice down.

"You have committed no crime. To be deported does not mean that you are a criminal, only a nuisance. We have an order to take you to the airport and send you back to London on the first available aircraft."

Stagg sipped at his coffee and watched the hard, green heads of the burgeoning sunflowers move in the breeze. He found it impossible to meet his mother's eyes.

"The manager at the hotel is obviously a very influential man," he said eventually. "I wish I'd known that."

"His son-in-law is the under-secretary to the Minister of the

Interior," the driver explained. "Now, my name is Yasouf and this is not my true brother, but my friend and comrade, Ali. We are both compassionate men."

"I'd like to say *enchanté*," Stagg muttered bitterly. "This is an outrage, you know. I will complain through the Foreign Office."

Ali touched Stagg's cuff and indicated with his eyes that he should look after his mother who had turned from the table and was looking at the ground.

"Are you all right?" Stagg asked her, getting to his feet.

"It's a bit of a shock . . . " Joyce quavered. "I thought I could handle it, but being sent home without getting up into the mountains, to come all this way . . . "

Ali took out a small black book from his pocket and riffled the pages.

"We are Muslims," he said. "There is an aircraft which leaves for London at ten-thirty tonight. We will drive you to the cemetery and deport you later. This will take all day, but it is a good act."

Stagg straightened his back. The immigration officers were in a silent accord, drinking their coffee and nibbling at cakes, glancing at him with shining, dark eyes, their book on the table between them. When he looked at Joyce he saw that she had accepted their offer without demurring, satisfied that her natural rights had been recognised.

"I'm grateful to you," Stagg said with measured respect, "and you have my admiration, but I will see to it that the manager gets no more tourists from Britain, in any way I can. He's a shit and should be shot."

Yasouf shook his fingers and blew on them as a sign that he thought Stagg's attitude was inflammatory and perilous, but he admitted a grin to his moustache.

"We have a very long way to travel before you can fulfill your oath of pilgrimage," he said grandly. "Our departmental car goes at two hundred kilometres an hour, if pressed. Are you ready?"

With grave and sober calm the immigration officers rose from their seats and stood either side of Joyce's chair. She allowed them to help her get up, then rested her hands on their proferred arms while they led her to the car. Stagg watched the little procession, unaccountably reminded of the Queen being led up the altar steps by solicitous bishops during her coronation at Westminster Abbey.

In order to prove the capabilities of the departmental car, Yasouf drove at very high speed along the stretch of road from Bir-Bou-Rekba to Grombalia, overtaking at risk, sounding his horn at every cart and lorry, shaking his fist at every vehicle which held him up. Stagg and Joyce sat in the back seat, determinedly oblivious.

"Yasouf is a good driver, but I am better," Ali said as the car nosed into a side-street in Grombalia and stopped in front of a tall, shuttered house. "We are just checking on our relatives here."

"Are you going to deport them as well?" Joyce asked chirpily.

"This is my uncle's house," Ali announced. "He has been a sick man for many years. Whenever I pass through Grombalia it is my duty to visit him."

A few minutes later Ali came out of the house and invited Stagg and his mother in to meet his uncle. The old man was exceptionally gaunt, sitting bolt upright in the corner of a room on a carpet, a fringed shawl around his bony shoulders. There was no life in his eyes which were small and pebble-shaped on either side of a huge hawk-nose.

"My uncle remembers your husband," Ali said. "His name was Stagg."

Joyce giggled, moving over to a window which had its shutter partly open. She was intrigued by the emptiness of the room. It had no furniture in it whatsoever and the walls were bare.

"Mr Stagg was a British soldier," Ali asserted confidently, his hand on his uncle's lumpy, shaven cranium which was as grey as limestone. "My uncle is unsure of his rank but from the beauty of his widow he assumes that he was a general."

Joyce shrieked with laughter. The old man looked heavenwards, raising his hand in protest. Ali made a gesture of resignation and led them towards the door.

49

"As you can see, my uncle is poor," he said in a low voice. "He lives off the alms given by the faithful."

Stagg stood his ground, his hands well away from his pockets, refusing to be drawn into an act of generosity. Ali shifted from one foot to the other, his features showing annoyance.

"There are earlier flights to London," he murmured.

"I can't give money to the relative of a man who is throwing me out of his country," Stagg replied. "If you're working on the principle that one good act deserves another you might as well take us straight to the airport. We have done no wrong, neither has your uncle. Let's leave it at that."

Ali scratched his head, leading them out into the street where a crowd of urchins had gathered round the car. He held out his arms to them and smiled whereupon they all ran away.

"The children." He uttered the word with a little sigh. "So many are hungry."

When they recommenced their journey Ali was the driver and he took it upon himself to demonstrate his superior skill as a motorist, coming so close to vehicles in front when trying to overtake that he repeatedly touched bumpers. Stagg protested at first but after the third such occasion he kept quiet, noticing that none of the other drivers involved seemed to be aggrieved. On the outskirts of Tunis, Ali drove up behind an articulated lorry carrying concrete pillars and ran the car beneath the overhang while braking too late at a set of traffic lights. In the confusion, the articulated lorry moved on when the lights changed to green, dragging the Citroën along. Eventually the driver heard the horn which Ali was desperately sounding and came to a halt. There was a kerbside discussion during which Ali and Yasouf flashed their identity cards at the driver of the articulated lorry, frequently pointing at the inhabitants of the rear seat, then Ali and Yasouf got back into the car, Ali hauling on the handbrake and pressing his foot down on the brake pedal as hard as he could, and the articulated lorry drew away, the concrete pillars tearing at the roof of the Citroën.

Once the car was free Yasouf got out and examined the damage. When he sat down in the passenger seat again his face was grave.

"That will take a lot of explaining," he told Ali as he drove on. "We have taken many chances so that these people in the back can venerate their dead."

Chapter Five

Joyce took little interest in the remainder of their journey to Madjez-el-Bab, her mind retreating from the peculiarly self-contained chaos which Stagg and the Tunisian immigration officers created between them. It did not seem to matter any more whether they went to the airport and stood parked at the entrance for half an hour while Stagg fumed at the unspoken threats of his tormentors, or that the drive from Tunis to Madjez-el-Bab proceeded in contradiction to the signposts, passing through small hill towns full of sheep and goats. A peace had settled on her spirit. She had relinquished her hold on the old imaginings she had had of this place, the buckled photographs, the letters her husband Frank had written to her from the battle in these mountains. Nothing was as she had thought it might be, and that was a boon. If she never saw the grave now, it was of little consequence. By their unsubtle antics and the simple cast of their cupidity, Yasouf and Ali had demilitarised her memory.

"Do you have a uniform?" she asked suddenly.

"We should have worn it today but it is at the dry-cleaners," Yasouf replied, pushing his fingers into his thick, curly hair. "Light blue, with a red stripe down the side of the trousers."

Joyce looked at the swathes of white and yellow spring flowers which lay over the foothills. Peasant women in brightly coloured cloaks and hats led donkeys along the roadside, purples and reds predominating. She noted the straightness of their features and their erect bearing.

"If you married a girl like that and took her back to England, what d'you think would happen?" she asked Stagg, unable to disguise the mischief in her tone.

Stagg tightened his lip, peeved that his mother had read his thoughts. It was a day-dream he often had, transplanting something or someone beautiful into his personal empire. These women with their bold, black eyes and brilliant apparel were a delight, crossing the pools of flowers like exotic fowl.

"After a few months they'd want to go home," he replied coldly. "We wouldn't be able to communicate."

"Would you marry one of these women, Ali?" Joyce asked.

He shook his head and explained that the tribe which these girls belonged to was not Islamic.

"What are they, then?"

"They are pagans."

Joyce put a finger on her lips and regarded the retreating figures out of the rear window with increased interest.

"I've never seen a pagan before," she said blithely. "This is my lucky day."

They went towards the market town of El-Fahs which was, Yasouf assured them, full of illegal immigrants from Algeria, but turned off left a few kilometres outside it and headed into wild, open country overhung by a sky full of blazing white clouds. Thirty minutes later Yasouf drove down a track bounded by high banks of ox-eye daisies, violets and vetch. In the distance Stagg could see great pillars standing darkly against a mountain.

"Are we at Dougga?" he asked.

"No, this is Thuburbo Majus. My cousin works here," Yasouf replied.

Stagg gazed at the site. It was broken and scattered, full of flowering bushes and small trees. There were no other cars parked at the entrance.

"Will you take a walk, madame?" Yasouf said as he opened the door. "Before we go to the British war cemetery I thought you should visit the Roman tombs. Everyone comes to Tunisia to fight, even in restaurants."

Joyce took Stagg's arm and walked behind the immigration

officers, along the uneven, overgrown path, puzzled but amused.

"Did you hear what he said to me, the cheeky devil?" she whispered. "He thinks we're hooligans."

"I'm afraid that we're in the hands of madmen," Stagg muttered. "I didn't want it to be like this. If you feel too upset to face it, let me know."

"I feel marvellous, honestly," Joyce replied heartily. "Don't ask me why but I do."

As they approached a line of free-standing pillars which had been the supports of a temple façade, a shaggy young man in a worn black suit climbed out of a cistern and greeted them effusively, a drop of moisture hanging from the end of his nose.

"This is my cousin," Yasouf said. "He is a professor. Please talk to him. His English is of a very high standard."

With a sinking heart Stagg listened to the professor's spiel on the history of the site, his eyes on the man's hands which were thrust into his jacket pockets. When they were withdrawn each held a bundle of cloth which, once unfolded, he saw contained old coins.

"Roman," the man declared like a conjuror.

"I could have one of those made into a pendant," Joyce said, fingering a large piece which glinted brassily.

"The Emperor Tacitus," the cousin proclaimed proudly. "How much?"

"There wasn't an emperor called Tacitus," Stagg gibed, pulling Joyce away. "You made that in your own back yard."

"There was an emperor called Tacitus," the professor insisted.

"Tacitus was an historian," Stagg shot over his shoulder as he steered Joyce back past the cistern. "Now leave us alone, will you?"

The man caught up with them and plucked at Stagg's sleeve. When Stagg wheeled round in a fury he saw that the fellow was trembling with emotion.

"I found this coin myself. It is worth a lot of money," he blubbered, wiping his nose on his sleeve. "Tacitus came after the joint emperors Quintillus and Aurelian and before Probus."

"Claptrap!" Stagg barked. "You've learnt that off by heart."

"Of course I have. How else would I know it?"

The man retreated, his disappointment and resentment clearly marked on his long, sad face. On their way back to the car, Yasouf and Ali stopped to talk. They patted his back and made showy gestures of resignation towards the car. Stagg watched, guessing what was passing between them, his anxiety on the increase.

"I hope I'm playing this right," he said, half to himself. "What these two are up to, I don't know."

"Perhaps it's just the way they go about things," Joyce answered, hoping to comfort him. "Son, if we're being deported anyway, what difference does it make how they go about it?"

"I'm worried in case they become really fed up with me. I'm not getting the message you see. This is a shake-down. I'm supposed to cough up for this trip. To be frank, I'm doubtful whether they're immigration officers at all."

"Then who are they? They've got those identity things."

"I would think everyone's got one of those in one form or another. They were in Arabic, probably video-club membership cards."

Joyce was silent. When Ali and Yasouf got back in the car she immediately started talking about her childhood and the Liverpool which had existed between the two world wars, the poverty which had ached in the streets of Everton, the unemployment and hardship. At the end of her description she remarked that it was her guess that everyone in the car had known, first hand, what it was to be poor.

"But we were clean," she added. "My mother used to stand beside her washing on a Monday afternoon with her chest stuck out, and she'd done it all by hand. Also, we were never hungry; she always found something. What a cook she was. My father used to give her a quarter of his wages and drank the rest, but she managed. And I'll tell you something else. My great-uncle Jack was a customs officer."

Yasouf and Ali listened attentively, their heads craned back to hear everything she said above the noise of the engine as the car howled down the long, straight Roman road off the mountain into the valley of the River Medjerda.

"Something which may surprise you," she asserted, persevering in her attempt to penetrate the sensibilities of her audience, "but I'm certain people were much happier; not only that, but people are still trying to be happy in that way, and that's a big mistake. Things have changed so much. There has to be a new way for people to be happy that isn't dependent on those memories. What do you boys think of that suggestion?"

"We are Muslims," Ali replied trenchantly. "We know how to be happy."

"Well, I'm ready to accept that, but I'm not sure it can last for ever. When I read the Koran it struck me that it was just like the Old Testament."

Ali decelerated, allowing the Citroën to cruise.

"You have read the holy Koran, madame?" Yasouf demanded.

"Yes," Joyce averred stoutly, "I have."

"Why did you do that?" Ali said, fondling the gear change.

"Because my son told me to."

"Ah," Ali sighed, changing back up to fifth gear. "This man is a seeker after truth. What is the Old Testament?"

"Part of our Bible," Stagg interjected, not wanting the exchange to touch on anything Jewish in case there might be political repercussions.

"We shall read the Old Testament, and our children will read it." Yasouf declared, "as long as it does not make us unhappy."

"What I'm saying, son, is we're all in the same boat. If you hang on for all you're worth to a book written in the desert more than a thousand years ago then you're going to get left behind."

The conversation had taken them through the squalid, muddy town of Madjez-el-Bab, over the Medjerda, and to the cemetery gates. Ali stopped the car. Before he got out, he turned to Joyce, pointing at the rank upon rank of white headstones which stretched away towards the dark mountains.

"Look about you if you wish to see those who have been left behind," he said. "We are here."

★

56

Stagg watched his mother, rapt. One glance at the cemetery had been enough to convey its orderly beauty. It was like the garden of a great English mansion, surrounded by a wall, sheltered by tall trees. Nothing could have been more of a shock to her, he decided. Whenever she had spoken of this place it had been in the most deprecatory way. It was linked in her mind with the shabbiness of her treatment as a war-widow. Now, as she stood at the gates, her protruding eyes open as wide as a child's, he withdrew a few steps from her. In the warm spring air many birds sang, their music identical to those in England. What will she say? he thought, his eye slipping past her isolated figure to the enormous wheatfields which flanked the cemetery, running to the base of the blue-grey mountains. She must crack, and speak.

"Which one is it?" she asked in a high voice, her hands twining the strap of her handbag into a bond.

Panic rushed into Stagg's blood. He felt in his pockets, looking for the papers from the War Graves Commission.

"I've got it somewhere," he muttered.

Joyce moved forward, apparently unconcerned, her head held far down as she peered at the headstones in the front rank.

"All these young men," she said. "Look at these lovely geraniums they've grown, and the quality of the grass. Isn't this a lovely spot, Malcolm?"

Stagg could not find the papers. In the confusion of their stay at the hotel he had left them in his other jacket.

"You wait here, Ma, and I'll find it," he said, setting out for the end of the first rank at a trot.

"Don't run in a graveyard, son," Joyce advised him. "It's unlucky."

Stagg slowed down, his heart hammering. He had wrecked the moment for her. He was going to spend the entire day looking for one grave in this vast necropolis, humiliated. Such stupidity and negligence! He cursed himself as he went from headstone to headstone, from pilot to bombardier to light infantryman to tankman, privates, corporals, sergeants, officers, the Surreys, the Inniskillins, the Royal Electrical and Mechanical Engineers, the Dragoons.

"Have you found him yet, son?" Joyce piped amongst the birds. "I thought you said there was a system."

Stagg's heart burned. All these names, these names! It would take him the rest of his life. 4432678/L/Cpl., 2375890/Flt. Lt., 1664785/Pte . . . Numbers, green as those on his computer screen, grass-green, reflecting red geraniums, shivered in his mind. He could not possibly get through all these graves to find his father.

"I'll start the other end!" Joyce shouted. "I'll get Ali and Yasouf to help. They're standing there doing nothing."

"No!" Stagg heard himself shouting. "I'll find him! Sit down and have a rest."

Joyce went and sat on a bench by the gates with the immigration officers and smoked a cigarette while Stagg slowly paced down the front rank, checking the information on each headstone. His gait was taut and controlled in contradiction to his feelings. With his mother's eyes on him and under the scrutiny of the Tunisians, in which he detected an element of mockery, Stagg would have rather run across the cemetery, leapt the wall and galloped through the wheatfield into the mountains.

Stagg.

He stopped, unable to believe his eyes. In the centre of the front rank, shielded by a large blood-red geranium, was his father.

3660683 CPL
F. W. STAGG
ROYAL ENGINEERS
1ST FEBRUARY 1943 AGE 26

"GOD PROVED HIM
AND FOUND HIM WORTHY
OF HIMSELF."

She's right, he thought, what the hell does that mean?

"Ma!" he roared. "He's here!"

Stagg walked backwards for a few steps, then turned to look at his mother. She was carefully stubbing her cigarette out on the concrete base below the seat.

"Looks as though Malcolm's found him already," she said to the immigration officers, "that's saved some time."

On her way over to take her son's arm which he had extended towards her, Joyce felt the world start to shake as it had done almost half a century ago when she had stood on a doorstep which she had been scrubbing and read a telegram notifying her of Frank's death. Once again she had to find a way of controlling the rivening grief, or fall apart.

"Right in the front," Stagg said to her. She noticed how his eyes were too bright and the strange nature of his smile. "The boy thinks he's bringing us back together again," Joyce whispered to herself.

She read the headstone, feeling a surge of ascending cold as she saw the inscription she had chosen. The headstones on either side had perfectly straightforward epitaphs selected by perfectly straightforward wives. What had bidden her pick such a conundrum to put over her husband's head?

Joyce shook her head regretfully.

"My heart feels like a block of ice," she said.

Stagg frowned, his own tears far too plenteous to hide.

"It's too long, son. Between you and me, I don't think he's under there anyway."

With a shock, she realised that her son, this man caught up in the military trappings of this place, needed harsh measures.

"Do you know how he died?" she demanded of him, hating the shine of his tears. "You may have forgotten your papers, Malcolm, but I've got mine. Here!" She opened her bag, took out an opened envelope and thrust it at him, then walked on, her head singing with sinister grief.

Stagg took the letter out of the envelope and read it. He discovered from its contents that his father had been killed with five others while unloading land-mines. The information had no effect upon him whatsoever. He followed his mother along the rank of headstones and returned the envelope.

"Thank you for letting me see that," he said politely.

"Well, you see what I mean?" Joyce raged suddenly.

"Mean what?" Stagg replied, concerned.

"I lied to you."

"No you didn't."

"I told you that he'd been killed by a land-mine!" Joyce cried, then shuddered as tears began.

Stagg moved away, sensing that she did not want him too close.

"He *was* killed by a land-mine," he said.

"But I didn't say it was an accident!" Now it was too late to pull back and she wept, angrily. "Because you were a little boy and we'd built him up to be such a hero."

Stagg guided his mother along an avenue of cypresses towards another seat and they sat down in the sun. He did not speak. Such was his strength at that moment that words would only serve to weaken him; the truth, that strange thing, was glowing within him and seemed to be in his sole possession.

"You don't mind?" Joyce asked him, putting a hand on his chest.

Stagg gave a tiny shake of his head, no more than a tremble of his existence.

"You're the only other person who knows," she went on. "I couldn't bring myself to tell anyone."

"You were ashamed?"

"Yes."

Stagg moved his feet backwards and forwards on the turf, observing a yellow and black caterpillar writhing round a blade of grass.

"Do you think that was right?" he asked eventually. "After all, the man died for his country. He was unloading land-mines in the middle of a battle. Land-mines had to be unloaded by someone. How do you know that he hadn't just returned from a bayonet charge?"

Stagg was amazed to hear the note of sarcasm in his voice. At this time? At such a moment?

"There was another letter," Joyce sobbed.

"Have you still got it?"

"No."

"What did it say?"

"It said that Frank had been the man in charge of the men unloading the land-mines."

60

"So?"

"They said that there'd been an investigation and Frank had been cleared of any suspicion of incompetence."

Stagg stood up and roared with laughter, opening his lungs so the burden could blow out of his mouth like a shell.

"Incompetence?" he yelled. "Look at this! Look at these poor bastards, in bits, and they talk about incompetence. The world was incompetent! For years and years. Have we got over it? Is there going to be a better time?"

The immigration officers came running down the avenue wagging their fingers at his desecration. By the time that they had reached the seat, Stagg was calm again.

"Nervous tension," he explained.

"You must behave respectfully," Yasouf reprimanded him.

"I apologise," Stagg said, but he could not help smiling still, the war in its clown's hat active in his mind. "When I'm overwrought, I laugh. It's in the family."

"Is this not a beautiful garden?" Ali said solemnly, his hand making a sweep over the cemetery. "People come here from all over the world to be with their relatives. This is a serious place, Monsieur Stagg, not an amusement park. Imagine the work that goes into keeping the garden so nice. Here are the workers, going about their daily business."

Two men in stained overalls appeared out of the hedge, one pushing a wheelbarrow. The other, the oldest, a stocky, bald-headed man with a dog-like expression, was carrying a long-handled spade and a wooden-toothed rake. As he walked along he hummed monotonously. The gardener with the wheelbarrow was no more than a boy. He pushed it up to where Joyce was sitting and parked it right at her feet.

"Your relatives seem to be anticipating a very heavy tip," Stagg said ill-naturedly.

Yasouf flashed him a glance composed of sorrow, exasperation and pity in equal parts, then sat down next to Joyce on the seat.

"These men are very poor, with large families," he said. "As good Muslims labouring in a Christian garden, they salute you."

The bald-headed gardener nodded and began raking at the grass around the seat. Stagg turned away from this beggar's dumb-show and returned to his father's grave, crouching beside it. The headstone he saw as a building from his own pen. Beneath the foundations was a cavern in the African rock where his father, Atlas-like, worthily held up a world unworthy of himself, thus fulfilling the epitaph in a curious way.

Upon his return to the car he found his mother counting out the entire contents of her purse on to the bonnet in two piles, the notes held under the thumbs of Ali and Yasouf. Once she had given the money to the gardeners who had been sitting on the wall, waiting, she asked Stagg to take a photograph of her with them, which he did, noting that the immigration officers were not willing to be included in the picture when invited to do so.

"Would you like me to take one of the grave?" Stagg asked Joyce as she disengaged herself from the gardeners.

"I'm not bothered. I've got those snaps the Army sent me," she replied. "To be honest, Malcolm, I got sick of looking at them."

"Don't you want one in colour, for the sake of the geraniums?"

"If you like."

Stagg returned through the gates. As he did so a mass of thundercloud rose over the eastern mountain, casting a cold shadow which flowed over the earth towards the cemetery. Beyond the town he could see Long Stop Hill, already dark and ominous. From his childhood memories he evoked imaginings of a cactus grove where, so he had been told years later when Joyce had forgotten that she had never informed him that his father was dead, the man had died. Until that time the family had persisted in lying to him that Frank was expected home any time; grandmother, grandfather, uncles and aunts all incapable of giving him the truth. With the camera in his hand he squinted through the viewfinder, his mind full of the spines in that cactus grove. The aspirin whiteness of the stone was no anodyne for the imagined pain, the shattered flesh of his father.

"They did what they could for him," he had heard his grand-mother say in the small parlour where the family had sat out the war; then, remembering the boy, she had added. "Frank's best friend, I mean, God bless him, you know, the one who was killed."

His hand would not keep still long enough to take the picture. He knelt down and put the camera on the grass, hoping to focus it on to the headstone from there. As he bowed over the camera, laying his head on the grass to look through the viewfinder, Yasouf and Ali came over and knelt beside him, their faces turned towards the birthplace of the Prophet. Stagg looked up at them through a curved glass of tears.

"Your mother has asked us to pray for your father with you," Ali said quietly, his forehead touching the grass, "which is, of course, forbidden as he was an infidel, but we are compassionate men."

Stagg and his mother were taken another forty kilometres to the west and presented to the relatives of the immigration officers at Dougga, the great Roman ruin, where it rained. Sullen men in damp burnouses followed Stagg and his mother along streets which were paved with wheel-rutted stone, pouring out histor-ical facts, and battered coins from sacks. Meanwhile, Stagg's heart hardened against his mother and her friendship with Ali and Yasouf. It was an act of weakness on her part, and a be-trayal. For a moment they left her alone while she was standing in the theatre erected by Marcius Quadrutus in 188 AD in Cor-inthian style. Stagg went swiftly to her side.

"Don't encourage them so much," he said *sotto voce*. "You're making things very difficult for me."

"I don't know what you're talking about," she replied. "They're nice lads, both of them. Look at this majestic panorama."

"They're paying you a lot of attention."

Joyce peered at herself in a puddle, touching strands of hair coquettishly. Stagg reacted violently, throwing his hands up.

"I knew it! You're egging them on," he fumed. "Be your age!"

"Madame will you see the house of prostitution now?" Yasouf said gallantly as he returned. "It is only a little walk."

Stagg barred his way, his long, sensitive fingers flexing anxiously on the lapels of his linen jacket.

"We should be getting back," he said agitatedly. "You've been very kind to bring us here and we appreciate it, but my mother mustn't get too tired."

"Are you tired, madame?" Yasouf asked.

"No, I'm having the time of my life," Joyce proclaimed. "Let's have a look at the house of prostitution."

Stagg miserably followed them down the rocky path, rain dripping down his collar. On either side were men with palms full of sestertes from Augustus to Maximinus intoning numismatic credentials. While Joyce explored the shattered, roofless chambers alleged to have been the setting for second-century debauchery, Stagg sat on a wet rock and stared at the array of blackened and twisted coins on offer. To divert his mind from its downward plunge he asked for prices and scoffed at those proposed by the vendors; but, at least, they were ambitious, rarified in their absurdity. As he haggled, he could not help feeling despondent at the rapid rate at which the prices were lowered, further proof, to him, that intrinsic value is a myth in this world.

"Why didn't you tell me that my father had been killed?" he called down into the ruined brothel where his mother was hard at work imagining what it must have been like to be a whore in those distant times. "Christ, he was dead before I was born!"

"I can't hear a word you're saying," Joyce shouted back as she entered a roofless chamber directly below where he was sitting.

"You can hear well enough when you want to!" Stagg roared down upon the top of her grey head, his heart shocked by the eruption of a great anger against his mother. "Can't you imagine what it was like for me, knowing and not being able to say? I felt a complete fool!"

"Oh, shut up moaning, Malcolm," came the reply from the dank excavations. "You've done all right."

"Everyone knew he was dead. The neighbours' kids were always telling me."

"Then what are you beefing about?" Joyce said crisply as she emerged into sunlight which had broken through the rain clouds.

"Because I had to pretend that I thought he was alive."

"Well, son, those were difficult times for all of us."

One of the vendors had reached an absurdly low price for an obvious forgery of a coin bearing a charioteer. Stagg gave him what he asked then tossed his purchase down at his mother's feet. If he had not had that gesture to fall back on he would have done something worse.

"Here's something to hang around your neck," he bellowed.

Joyce picked it up and looked at him.

"What do you know about anything," she said with resolute dignity, climbing up broken steps towards him. "What do you know about those days?"

"I know that you left me to suffer the worst deprivation there is," Stagg replied, his eyes like coals.

"I made you into a man, somehow, didn't I? You're a success, I think, so don't go blaming me for all that old pain. I don't remember not telling you that your father was dead, but if I didn't it was for your own good."

Stagg laughed at her outrageous claim, staring at the woman's gleaming face and bedraggled hair as if she were a pitiless harpy who had ascended from the infernal regions.

"It was years before you'd talk about him as if he were dead," he seethed, "and then it was only so you could claim that I was half an orphan and put me in for a scholarship to that bloody boarding-school."

"Now, now, Malcolm," Joyce murmured, "let's not go into that."

"Yes, let's go into that!" Stagg retorted loudly, his manner so aggressive that he created a ripple effect amongst the encircling Arabs. "You wanted to get shot of me. They thrashed me day in day out."

"That's a terrible thing to say," Joyce said weakly, sitting down on

65

a step opposite him, her face collapsing into a mask of suffering. "I would never have allowed you to be beaten by anyone."

Stagg paused, his ears ringing. He was aware that he had said something so unjust and cruel that he could not apologise for it. There was an untruth so large lodged in his accusation that even the truth could not lever it out. He had said it. The lie had come from somewhere. What sort of man am I? He asked himself as he saw the damage he had done. But within it had been something she should know.

"That's the worst thing I've ever said to you," he admitted sternly, newly aware of his public as they reconvened closely around him. "I withdraw it unconditionally. All I can do is ask forgiveness."

Which she gave, or said she gave.

Stagg and his mother were deported with a certain degree of ceremony on a delayed holiday charter flight from Tunis airport at one-thirty in the morning. The drive back from Dougga had taken them to le Kef near the Algerian border where Ali and Yasouf had insisted upon buying a prayer-mat for each of them, the work of belligerent tribal weavers who traditionally ignored all frontier regulations, crossing the national boundaries with impunity, thereby earning the Islamic esteem of the immigration officers. Stagg had been unwilling to accept the gift, knowing the expectations it would create once the time came for Yasouf and Ali to take their leave; but his mother had dismissed his reservations as churlish and unmanly.

"They deserve every penny," she said as Stagg counted out the Tunisian currency on the top of the desk in the airport immigration office. "The money you saved when we were shown the door of the hotel will do. What's a few hundred pounds to someone with all you've got? They're poor. Give it to them."

"It's a lot of money," Stagg muttered. "They'll laugh themselves sick once we've gone. They've taken me to the cleaners."

"No, they haven't," Joyce assured him. "They looked after us, drove us everywhere, introduced us to people, bought us presents . . . "

"All right, all right," Stagg said, handing one bundle of notes to Yasouf and the other to Ali. "Here, chaps. And thanks for literally everything. I don't know what we'd have done without you."

"There is one thing," Ali said solemnly as the folded banknotes disappeared into his hip pocket. "We need your passports."

Stagg and his mother handed them over. Ali opened a double-locked wall cupboard and revealed a rack of blue-handled rubber stamps.

"Deported, deported, deported," he said under his breath, his forefinger searching down the row. "Ah, this is the one."

He took the stamp out of the rack, flipped up the lid of an ink-pad, pressed the stamp hard on to the surface, opened the two passports at a blank page, then held the stamp over them.

"Mr Malcolm Stagg, British Subject: Citizen of the United Kingdom and Colonies, 435621 E: Occupation, architect: *Lieu de naissance*, Liverpool: Distinguishing marks, nil: (PAUSE) Give us your blessing."

Stagg saw the light in the man's eyes. It was not a twinkle but a gleam of Damascene steel. To have his passport stamped this way would be a hindrance to his business. At home he had existing contracts in Jordan and Syria. Not to be able to travel freely in the Arab world would cripple him, professionally.

"What does my blessing matter?" he replied, equivocating warily. "Surely a benediction from an atheist is worthless?"

"Give it to us as a man who forgives his mother his birth," Ali replied, "and as a possessor of wealth, fortune and talent. Joyce is proud of you for some reason. Give me your hand."

As Stagg held out his hand Ali took it and forcefully pressed the stamp on to the back.

"In the time it takes to wash that off," he said, "grow up."

Chapter Six

The seven days after their return from Tunisia were as disturbing to Stagg as the days of the Creation were to the Void, each one full of shocks and transformations in his mother's moods. She was exhilarated one moment, downcast the next, active then inert, gloomy then high on optimism, argumentative then conciliatory, all in a swirl of strange behaviour which went with her presence like a dust-devil. He could not keep up with her and, truth to tell, he did not try too hard because within himself he was feeling a sense of well-being, a constantly benign, unquestioning gladness about having successfully completed the pilgrimage.

As time went by these alternations of mood in Joyce steadied up, veering markedly towards the negative as they lost their wild energy. She became cantankerous, then morbid, then silent, only talking to Mrs Hankinson, never choosing to share her thoughts with her son. Hilbre had been designed with a perfect acoustic in each room and conversation carried. When Joyce and Mrs Hankinson were in the kitchen or sitting on the edge of the indoor pool, Stagg could hear them whispering. Words reached his ears which were to do with graves and cemeteries, grief and loss, and the women laughed, which upset him.

Day by day he became more estranged from his mother, isolated in his own house by her conspiratorial foolishness. He felt it keenly and was hurt by her insensitivity in doing this to him so soon after such an adventuresome, emotional experience, one which he thought they had shared. But instead of bringing his mother closer to a world which she had scorned, the journey to see her husband's resting-place seemed to have driven her further away from reality, at least from his reality, which Stagg was certain was the true one.

One afternoon his mother pushed her way through the anatomical swing-doors of the gymnasium as Stagg was performing his daily routine of strenuous exercises. She stood watching him for several minutes as he did a vigorous hip-roll with dumb-bells and the melancholy derision in her eyes made him stop short of the fifty rotations which he had set himself.

"Are you all right?" he asked, prickled by her attitude.

"No, I'm not all right, I'm not all right at all," she replied. "You've seen the way I've been behaving."

Stagg was stuck for a rejoinder. He slumped his shoulders as part of a loosening-up exercise which prepared his upper torso for work on the wall-bars.

"Yes, I'd noticed," he said in a dry voice.

"Then why didn't you say something?"

Stagg flexed his fingers and looked up at the glass roof. It was etched with Attic athletic figures. More than anything he wanted to get on with his exercises. In his inner mind he knew that his mother was struggling both to apologise and ask for his help but his yearning to take refuge in his physical routines was too strong. He climbed up the wall-bars, hooked his feet between them and hung upside-down.

"Will you listen to me, please?" Joyce asked plaintively.

"I must keep my momentum going," Stagg gasped, his face going red. "It's all right. I can carry on talking."

"I only want a minute to explain . . . " Joyce stammered, tears in her eyes. "Don't be indifferent, Malcolm."

Stagg pulled himself up into a right angle, his teeth clenched.

"Just let me do three of these," he hissed. "Then we can sort everything out. It won't take long."

Joyce turned away and sat on a bench by the window while he finished raising and lowering his long, once-lean frame. When he got down off the wall-bars and came over to her, she could not look at him.

"That was to teach me a lesson, wasn't it?" she said.

69

"I have my own life, Ma," he replied. "It's always worth remembering that. Now, what can I do for you?"

He sat down next to her and waited. After a while she opened her heart to him, confessing that she was full of doubts about whatever good he had imagined might come from the visit to Tunisia. She only had her feelings to go on and they were now full of confusion and resentment. The underlying result of the pilgrimage had been, as far as she was concerned, destructive.

"It's made me think that I've wasted my life since the war," she said grimly, "that I've been an absolute fool. That's left me feeling not as tough as I thought I was."

She got to her feet and Stagg saw that she was so shaky that she needed help. As his hand went out to support her she knocked it away.

"That doesn't mean that I can't stand on my own two feet!" she snapped. "You get on with what you were doing that was so important."

Then she left him to his regular mortifications.

Some days later Joyce said that she thought it would help if she visited Cissy, her younger sister, in Liverpool. This would recognise her need to share her experiences in Tunisia with someone who had known Frank in his heyday and could put it all in perspective.

Cissy lived on a run-down private estate adjacent to a new industrial complex, her front windows overlooking a freezer trade supplier's premises. Her husband, Les, worked for this company and lived a triangular existence between home, his place of employment over the road, and the Blue Anchor four doors away. When Joyce arrived after a frustrating rail journey across the wide waist of England, Les was sitting in a lime-green velour armchair watching television, eyes half-closed like the Buddha.

"Hello there, Joyce," he said, raising a hand, "I'll be with you in a minute. I just want to watch the end of this programme."

"You go ahead, Les," Joyce replied with genial sarcasm, "don't mind me. I've only been half-way round the world."

Les grinned and twitched his ponderous head sideways to indicate that he had understood the dig, then relaxed back into the armchair.

"He's been working two hours overtime every day, and Sundays," Cissy explained, bringing in a micro-waved lasagna and a can of strong lager to put beside him. "He's overdoing it. Let's talk in the kitchen."

Joyce lost no time in spreading her brochures and postcards on the kitchen table and opening her notebook.

"We stayed at the best hotel," she announced. "The plasterwork was amazing."

"Well, Malcolm's such a big deal he can afford to spoil you," Cissy said as she plugged in the electric kettle. "How was the cemetery?"

"Do you know, until I actually looked at the grave I didn't ever believe Frank was dead; not in my heart," she commented, treating herself as an objective study in order to subdue her impulse to brag to her sister. "It was an odd feeling. In my rational mind I knew he was dead but because I'd never seen the place . . . "

"Oh, that was all romance," Cissy interrupted with a mirthless smile. "You were always up to your necks in Hollywood, you and Frank."

"Were we?" Joyce asked, feeling dangerous. "I don't remember that."

"Oh, yes," Cissy sighed with an impatient shake of her head. "You were playing games. There was never anything realistic about you and Frank. You never got off the dance floor, really."

"Well, I never knew you had such an opinion." Joyce smiled winterily. "Sometimes I used to suspect that you were a bit jealous of Frank but then I'd say to myself, no, not Cissy. She's too good."

"Frank always fancied himself too much for my liking," Cissy continued in her own train of thought, sweeping up the age-encrusted allegation in the process. "All those clothes which he couldn't afford. Borrowing money. And always looking at himself in the mirror. That was never my kind of man."

Joyce raised a thumb at the intervening door.

"Is that your kind of man?" she enquired silkily.

"You would have done better to just sit down and face the truth when it happened," Cissy said, moving the subject back to more advantageous ground. "Everyone was too indulgent towards you. There were plenty of other women losing their husbands and they managed, somehow, but you had to be the queen of tragedy. That's what Dad called you, and he was right. People of our sort have to be tough."

"Tunis is Carthage," Joyce pronounced after taking a deep breath. "They worshipped the god Baal. Here's a picture of him."

Cissy's unseeing eye fell on the illustration.

"I don't want to sound unsympathetic, love, but I think you've wasted your life. You should have got married again. That's what Malcolm always wanted. I can remember him saying so . . . " Cissy paused for breath, her blood tingling as she saw the umbrage rising in her sister's expression. She had done well to get in first. If she had submitted to Joyce's perpetuation of melodramatic obsequies for the long-dead Frank it would have been a lengthy session. "Staying a widow was all very well, love, but hardly practical. You're not a hero or a martyr, you know. No one's going to put your name in the paper."

Joyce looked at her notebook and carefully ticked off a couple of items on a list.

"It was a very cruel religion," she lilted painfully. "They used to sacrifice their own children to the idol. And the scenery! Well, from this Roman city in the mountains called Dougga, funny name isn't it? you could see for miles, all the colours. I bought you a present; it's in my case . . . "

Cissy put a hand on top of Joyce's to halt the flow.

"I've always been straight with you," she said, manoeuvring for her sister's eyes to meet her own. "You've left everything too late, Joyce. This was a wild idea of Malcolm's and I don't think any benefit came of you going to see Frank's grave. It was pointless after all this time. If you'd wanted to go then it should have been straight after the war, but you didn't have the money, not on a war-widow's pension, I know — eighteen shillings a week, you told us how much often enough."

Joyce sat with her chin propped up on her elbows and listened to her sister, watching her wrinkled lips as if they were the jaws of a snake preparing to disgorge the contents of its poison sacs. She had believed that her sister would alter her views once the pilgrimage to Tunisia was accomplished. The pressure for her to behave in a conciliatory way would be irresistible. Joyce had looked forward to a new friendship which would take them into old age with affection and dignity.

"Are you all right?"

Cissy was staring at her, her eyebrows lifted with concern.

"Yes," Joyce answered, "I was just remembering the cemetery and the flowers. It's kept very tidy. I'd expected it to be in the desert, somehow. The Arabs have looked after it very well."

"Well, I expect they get paid to do that," Cissy said. "From what Frank said in his letters I thought they were very dirty people."

Joyce gloomily stirred the brochures and postcards with her finger, her lips pressed tightly together. The violence of Cissy's insults against Frank and herself were almost hallowed by tradition but the mean-minded nature of her remarks about the gardeners upset her. This was the old world. Nothing had changed. Words which had become freshened in her mind, long absent from her daily vocabulary — humanity, liberty and equality — limped back to the classroom.

"Didn't Hannibal come from Carthage?" Cissy spoke out of a spasm of regret, assembling a placatory grin. "The one with the elephants?"

"Yes, he did," Joyce replied, turning a booklet about Roman mosaics until it was the right way up. "Fancy you remembering that."

"I'm not completely stupid!"

The needle-sharp bristling of her sister made Joyce realise that her train journey, which had included three changes and an overall delay of an hour and twenty minutes, had been futile. Cissy thrived on resentment. She, herself, had reverted to type, victim and heroine. They were locked in an old, ritual rivalry.

"I didn't say you were stupid, love," Joyce said with an uneasy smile. "Sorry, I get carried away. It was so exciting out there."

"Well, it would be as well if you remembered that I've been stuck here with that!" Cissy suddenly flared up, pointing a finger at the door to the sitting-room where the television droned on. "Don't talk to me about the god they sacrificed children to." Then she broke down, her hands over her face, declared that she could not go on.

Joyce sighed; the only attempt at sympathy she could produce.

"What d'you care?" Cissy spluttered, her hand reaching out for the kitchen towel. "No one else is supposed to suffer but you."

"Cissy, every time I come here to have a chat you do the same thing. We have to talk about you," Joyce said with a senior's patience, "I've just come back from seeing Frank's grave in Africa, the biggest adventure of my life and you want to moan about your *husband*! I've not had a husband for fifty years. Try and remember that, will you?"

"Then you're a lucky woman!" Cissy exclaimed bitterly.

Joyce could not help inhaling a breath of triumph through her nostrils. "But I had Frank when he was at his best," she said, the thought emerging from an image of her mother comforting her, saying for the hundredth time that when men get sent off to war they never come back the same, her sharp Irish eyes grimly fixed on the drunk slumped by the fire, her father. "And Malcolm was only keeping his promise," Joyce added. "He always said he'd take me to Africa, and now he's done it."

"Your Malcolm always had a big head," Cissy averred, her waxen cheeks tinged with pink. "He was never one of us. You let him get above himself. I'll say this, Joyce, none of my kids have been divorced three times!"

"They haven't got the bloody life in them to get divorced!" Joyce hissed, sweeping all her brochures into a pile. "They might as well have been born in a vacuum-pack and kept in the freezer."

"You've been happy enough in the past to have what Les brought

74

home from work for you," Cissy came back at her, eyes popping with the family's thyroid power. "Don't sneer at us, Joyce. I won't have that. We're as good as you."

"Huh!" Joyce growled, marching to the door. "You're not worth bothering about. Thanks for helping me come to terms with seeing where Frank is buried. I believe he's dead now, as dead as you and that lump of lard next door. I can stop worrying about the lot of you."

Her case was still in the hall. Without calling in to say farewell to the dormant Les who was prone in front of a nature film about the last herds of American bison, Joyce went out of the front door and slammed it behind her, then hastened off down the street.

She returned in chastened mood ten minutes later and knocked firmly on the door. When Cissy opened it she was sniffing and red-eyed, a ball of sodden kitchen-towel in her hand.

"What do you want?" she croaked.

"Let's make up," Joyce suggested as she put her case over the threshold. "That was all a big mistake."

"I don't know where I am with you, Joyce," Cissy whimpered. "Whenever you come here we end up arguing." But she did not open the door to admit her sister, keeping it pressed up against the suitcase.

"We can start all over again," Joyce said soothingly, her head peering round the door. "Come on, love, let me in."

"No, I don't want you in this house ever again; not after what you said about Les and me being as dead as Frank."

"I was only joking."

"Les!" Cissy called out as Joyce pushed against the door. "Come out here, quick!"

Joyce heaved the door and Cissy aside and got in, snagging her tights on the lock of her suitcase as she did so. Cissy retreated to the foot of the stairs and sat down, distraught. The door to the sitting-room opened and Les stood blinking, his torpid responses galvanised by Cissy's alarm-call.

"What's up?" he mumbled sleepily.

"Our Joyce won't get out," Cissy lamented bitterly. "She's driving me mad again."

"How long have I been asleep?" Les murmured, rubbing at his gummed-up eyes. "I thought she'd only just arrived, or have I lost track?"

"She's insulted me!" Cissy shrieked as she went backwards up a few stairs on her rear. "Do something about it!"

"Not again," Les groaned. "Why don't you two sort yourselves out? Why do I have to get involved?"

"And she insulted you as well. She said you were dead."

Les shrugged and leant against the door-jamb.

"Well, she's right, isn't she?" he said with a loose grin. "Come on, Joyce, be fair. Make your mind up. Are you coming or going?"

"She's going! I never want to see her again as long as I live!" Cissy raved. "All she came here for was to make me feel little."

Les looked at Joyce and nodded his head towards the door.

"We'd better go. I'll run you to the station."

"You will not! Let her walk!" Cissy screeched.

Les picked up Joyce's suitcase and ushered her out, then closed the door behind them. As they drove away in his car Joyce saw the sad face of her sister at the bedroom window, and it was the face of a child.

Les dropped her off at Lime Street Station. He had been ready to park the car and carry the suitcase to the platform but Joyce persuaded him not to, preferring a quick goodbye at the setting-down strip of the station entrance. Once he had gone, she went to the escalator leading to the underground system and bought a ticket for West Kirby, travelling under the River Mersey on a crowded rush-hour train.

With her suitcase clenched between her knees, she strap-hanged most of the half-hour journey, remembering the thousands of trips she had made on the route during her working life. These were the same people in the form of a different generation. The rhythm had not shifted, the pattern remained. The train was a shuttle on the loom of her old life, still travelling backwards and forwards, weaving her absence into the design. This repetition had often had a

76

sustaining effect when the family had proved to be inadequate, so she did not hate the train, only the dim communion of suffering. There was always the end of the journey, the walk in the fresh air smelling the sea, the moment of relaxation with her mother when the daily motion of her life had ceased and rest supervened. Such an existence had been a good hiding-place, incorporated into the fabric of the universal working day, one of many, except for the raw, angry grief which had pulsed beneath every feeling she had and kept her separate.

As the train approached West Kirby she began to doubt the wisdom of her decision to revisit the scene of so many of her years. Already she was contrasting herself in her present state with the widow who had found a tranquilliser for her grief in routine, a routine which helped her to suppress nature and youth so she would not have to betray her dead husband. Was the impulse which had made her return to this hub of the past's machinery one of fear? Was she looking for the security of a dead time, where nothing could change, preferring that to the life she had now, so open and defenceless? From the memories she would encounter, she had only the protection of her new self; a self which the woman who had ridden this train twice daily for so many years would have ridiculed.

When the train arrived Joyce did not follow her old route to the house; instead she took a taxi down to the promenade and booked in at a guest-house overlooking the islands. The tide was going out. From the hall of the guest-house she made a telephone call to Norfolk but got the answering-machine which always struck her dumb. This evening it was especially unnerving to hear Malcolm's voice at the other end and know that he was not there in the flesh but merely part of the equipment. She put the telephone down sharply as soon as the answering message began but as she looked through the glass panel of the door at the shining sands she snatched the receiver up again and put the coins back into the box. When the answering-machine had finished its reply and she had obediently waited for the bleep, Joyce left her son this message:

"Malcolm, it's Joyce. I did as you suggested and read *Childe*

77

Harold's Pilgrimage on the train and, I must say, it was quite an eye-opener. Byron certainly seems to have had an exciting life if you believe everything he says about himself, and if he is Harold as you say he is. Also he seems to be guilty about something. Is that why you asked me to read the poem on the train?"

The money ran out and her contact was broken. Joyce rapped on the box with frustration then rang the operator to get a reverse charge call which was eventually refused because answering-machines have no such generosity. The landlady was clattering pans in the kitchen so Joyce went in and asked her for change to continue her call, returning with a handful. Once she had regained the ear of the answering–machine she pressed on with what she had wanted to say.

"I've taken note of the verses which made sense to me. Now, bearing in mind what you said about him treating people badly but having a rich life and a great spirit, was this all to do with how he coped with guilt? Is that what he made his poems out of? Did you mean to make such a pointed remark? Why did he have to give us a guided tour of all the ruins in Portugal and Spain and Greece and Italy to say what he wanted? What was the matter with English ruins? We've got plenty, which brings us back to me. I withdraw that, unconditionally. I know you hate it when I run myself down. I'm not a ruin, I'm mentally in my prime, so you say. Well, it's come at an odd time, son. I don't trust it completely. Aren't these emotions of mine some kind of cowardice? Shouldn't I grow old with dignity? Right now I feel as though I've been fooling myself lately. This will make you angry with me, Malcolm, I know, but I had to have someone to talk to. Forgive me for getting in another state. Where are we now? Hold on; don't go away." She clamped the receiver between shoulder and cheek while leafing through her notebook, squinting at her scribble to decipher it in the dim light of the solitary forty watt bulb overhead. "Now, I want you to write this down and we'll talk about it when I get home. I understand some of it but I'm not confident that I've got the full gist. It's me to a T.

Yet must I think less wildly: — I *have* thought
Too long and darkly, till my brain became,
In its own eddy boiling and o'erwrought,
A whirling gulf of phantasy and flame:
And thus, untaught in youth my heart to tame,
My springs of life were poisoned. 'Tis too late!
Yet am I changed; though still enough the same
In strength to bear what time can not abate,
And feed on bitter fruits without accusing Fate.

Son, did you tell me to read *Childe Harold's Pilgrimage* so that I'd
have to come across that verse? If you did then I can tell you that I
had to wade through a lot of inferior stuff to get to it. All those
exclamation marks. This! and That! But I like what he writes even
though we'd have never got on face to face. That poem is from the
Third Canto, verse seven, but you can't look it up because I've
borrowed your copy so it will have to wait. Well, I'm going out for
a drink with Cissy now. Les has agreed to make the dinner so we
can have a few hours together to see if we can put things on a better
footing in future. She's my blood, after all, the only drop of it left
except for you. I'll go now . . . " She hesitated, not wanting to
break off. "Don't ring back, son. You mustn't worry about me. I'm
as safe as a mad dog, as they say. Joyce! Byron would put at the start
of a poem about me. Intrepid traveller! Honourable dame!" With a
brief, self-conscious laugh she put the receiver down, then heard a
coin being returned, unused. She still had 20p. Who can I ring local?
she thought, then leant against the wall, chilled to the heart.

No one. After thirty years of living here. No one!

It had been her intention to go for a walk along the sands but the rain
came, keeping her in the guest-house. She had dinner in the bay
window of the small dining-room, her eyes gazing through the
dusk at the islands as they dissolved into the darkness. This was a
stupid move of mine, coming here, she said to herself while sawing
at a piece of pork too tough for her dentures. What the hell was I

doing? This is a wasteland. What was I looking for? The prospect of sleeping in the town once again horrified her. That bed, alone, the stillness of her flat where even a kitten was denied her by the regulations. She crossed her knife and fork on the plate in an act of exorcism, staring at the crucifix she had made out of the cheap metal cutlery.

"I'll believe in God again," she said over the plate. "I used to when I was a girl. It helped me, up to a point." Byron's notes to *Childe Harold's Pilgrimage* came back to mind. He had called Christianity an "execrable superstition", which echoed her own opinion. Was all that learning a superstition? A wrong religion, perhaps. Now, in a fearful moment of loneliness, she thought how cold and arrogant this condemnation was. When Frank had died she had gone to church; everyone in the family had gone to church. As she had sat in the pew, her mother had held her hand. The ritual had comforted her and calmed the unborn.

"Have you finished?" the landlady asked, her worn finger on the edge of the plate.

Joyce made no reply, her gaze fixed on the woman's finger. It was from the hand of her mother, discreetly exposed by the undertaker as she lay in her coffin in the front room, proof of a lifetime of hard work. Joyce remembered how effective it was as a reminder of the true nature of life for a woman of her mother's background; tedium, travail, drudgery. But her mother had been much more than that, rising above her destiny; and she, herself, was more than her lost decades. The image of the worn hand was evidence of strength, not submission.

"Excuse me, are you leaving what's on your plate?" The landlady was peering concernedly into Joyce's face which had become vacant and abstracted.

"No, I was just having a breather," Joyce replied, picking up her knife and fork again. "I was brought up to eat everything that was put in front of me."

After dinner she went for her walk, watched the last rays of the sun colouring the sheets of sea-water which lay like flakes of mica on the brown sand, had a drink at a pub and watched television in the saloon bar for half an hour, then strolled back to the guest-house feeling that she had weathered a storm. With the practised speed of a servant taking a vase off a shelf to expertly dust it down and put it back exactly where it had been, she had picked up faith then rejected it again, leaving the whole of eternity in as much isolation as she had suffered herself.

To the strange bed she went, falling asleep with the calmness of the windless sea, and dreamt about a giant answering-machine with a broken tape, the loose end of which whirled round in perpetual motion, flailing her beloved son in punishment for the trifling sins of his youth.

Chapter Seven

Stagg came home from a weekend conference in Harrogate on Sunday evening to find his mother entertaining Mrs Hankinson to dinner. As he stood in the antechamber of the warped rhombus which was the dining-room, looking through the scrollworked glass doors, he saw the two women in their finery, both flushed and lively, and their merriment gave him a jealous pang. In their cries of delight at his arrival Stagg thought that he detected a note of sardonic humour.

"We were only just talking about you, Malcolm," Mrs Hankinson said, two spots of colour glowing on her pale, slightly concave cheeks, "and here you are as if by magic. How did the conference go?"

Stagg was taken aback by the directness and familiarity of the daily help's tone. For a moment he could think of no way of dealing with the situation so he shrugged and murmured that the weekend had been bearable.

"And what was the conference about, son?" Joyce asked, adjusting the strap of her emerald satin dress, a garment which Stagg had never set eyes on before.

Stagg told her that the general title had been "Harmonius Urban Development", but the discussion had ranged further.

"I'd have thought that subject would require your total concentration," Mrs Hankinson said severely. "When you consider the mess that you architects have made of things it strikes one that there should be a five-year conference in Harrogate, not just a weekend."

Stagg carefully poured himself a glass of wine and thrust his long legs out under the table.

"Architecture has always created messes," he said levelly, giving Mrs Hankinson a cool, reproving stare which was designed to bring her to her senses, and her proper place. "There was never a time when every building was beautiful. In fact, Mrs Hankinson I'd say that architecture is as full of mistakes as the personal behaviour of most human beings."

"Oooooh!" Mrs Hankinson breathed. "Is that a fact?"

In the face of the daily help's facetiousness, Stagg fell silent. His mother blinked across the table at him and straightened her back as the chill descended.

"Moira has been talking to me about my ambiguous feelings," she declared, "and it's been very helpful."

Stagg waited for her to continue but she did not do so. From what he could interpret in her expression she expected Mrs Hankinson to pick up the thread and explain further on her behalf.

"And what ambiguous feelings are those?" Stagg asked, anxious to block any further access into the conversation for Mrs Hankinson.

"Moira will tell you," Joyce replied. "It took her a long time to winkle them out of me, didn't it?"

Mrs Hankinson nodded but she kept quiet, her eye on Stagg.

"Aren't you able to tell me yourself?" Stagg said.

"Well, you're a bit hard on me sometimes," Joyce giggled, but he caught the quaver in her voice. "I find it difficult to talk to you. Did you listen to me on the answering-machine?"

Stagg nodded. He had gone to a Harrogate book shop and bought a new copy of Byron's collected works on the strength of the rambling message he had received via his remote interrogator. It had been sandwiched between calls from Estoria, the United States, and Birmingham City Council and, in this company, Stagg had found what she had to say poignant.

"I'm glad that you read Byron as I suggested," he said, "and I see what you're saying about that verse applying to you."

"Yes, but let's not talk about that any more," Joyce rejoined, her

83

fingers fluttering in a dismissive gesture. "I've got beyond all that."
She held her breath. He could see that she was anxious about what
she was going to say.

"Go on, Joyce," Mrs Hankinson whispered, stretching over and
touching her hand, "don't be afraid."

Stagg's ire rose and he icily advised Mrs Hankinson to stop
prompting his mother.

"Why shouldn't she?" Stagg's mother reproached him. "She's
the only friend I've got down here. If it wasn't for her I wouldn't
have anyone to talk to most of the time."

Mrs Hankinson got to her feet and took a shawl off the back of
her chair.

"I'll go if it will help," she said nobly. "All that matters is that you
two thrash this out between you. I'm only a bystander."

"Don't say that about yourself," Joyce exhorted her, meanwhile
abandoning her chair to drape the shawl around Mrs Hankinson's
narrow shoulders. "You're far more than that."

"Well, I don't think everyone in the room appreciates me as
much as you do, Joyce. I'll leave you to it, I think. See you in the
morning. *Au revoir.*"

With that Mrs Hankinson blew two kisses, turned on her heel
and tottered out of the door.

Stagg got up and shut it firmly after her.

"That woman's drunk," he said upon his return.

"Of course she is. So am I."

"You needn't sound so proud of it."

"Nothing stops you getting drunk when you want to, does it?"

Stagg shrugged and sat down heavily.

"I don't enjoy this kind of hostility from you," he said in a
grumbling, fatigued tone, "especially in front of outsiders."

"She's not an outsider. Moira's told me all about herself. She's
sacrificed a great deal for the men in her life and is still waiting to be
paid back. She no longer feels love but she experiences passion."

Stagg was silent as he threaded his way through this elaborate
insight. It had a bearing upon the subject which he intended to raise
with his mother, something personal to himself but related in

nature to the predicament which Mrs Hankinson had made so interesting.

"Well, there is something important which I wanted to talk to you about but I don't think now's the best time," he said after a while.

Joyce perkily encouraged him to speak up. She was, she told him, ready for an all-night session if necessary and could he open another bottle?

Stagg sighed distractedly and shook his head, thrusting his hands into his pockets. "No, it's a touchy subject," he muttered. "We'd get into deep water."

"I've been in deep water all night. If you knew what Moira has told me it would make your hair stand on end."

Stagg bridled, lifting his head to glare at his mother.

"I'm talking about something which affects *us*, not the cleaning woman," he said sharply. "It will have to wait. I'm going to bed. Good night."

Joyce propped her chin on her elbows and, with some bravura, told him that he could do what he liked.

"Since I shared all my thoughts with Moira I've felt so much better," she added. "Up until tonight I've been quite miserable but now I feel I can go on."

Stagg winced, then raised a doubting eyebrow.

"Is it really as serious as all that?"

"You haven't bothered to discuss what happened to me out there in Tunisia, have you? You've left me to get on with it."

"I thought that you needed time to absorb everything," Stagg protested. "I would have talked to you at any time."

"Well, I haven't absorbed it. It's lying on me like a weight. I tell you, Malcolm, I'm running out of patience with you. You've got no sympathy. You make no attempt to put yourself in my place."

Stagg slumped back in his chair with a rattling groan and passed both hands over his thick, brown hair.

"Is this what you've been sharing with Mrs Hankinson?" he said. "Really, Joyce, it's a bit thick telling the cleaner before me."

"She helped to sort out a few things."

"Like what?"

"Why I came back feeling so guilty. Why you insisted on taking me out there in the first place. Why I'm all at sixes and sevens."

"She's been pretty busy then. I hope she spends as much time and energy cleaning the house."

Joyce fingered a thin gold chain around her neck and slowly pulled the brassy fake Roman coin out of the front of her dress and swung it in front of Stagg's nose.

"Moira says that you meant this to be a talisman of my wasted years. I had it done while I was up in West Kirby. The jeweller put the hole straight through the charioteer's head," she said meanly; then, with unsteady dignity, she rose from her chair, the coin still swinging from her fingers.

"Yes, Malcolm, I can say quite definitely that by taking me to Tunisia you have desiccated my entire life," she whispered hoarsely.

"Desiccated?" Stagg echoed. "Are you sure that's what you mean?"

"Exactly," she replied aloofly, colliding with the back of his chair as she headed for the door. "Just like a coconut."

Stagg's mother was sitting at the crescent-shaped marble table in the breakfast orangery when Stagg came down at six the following morning. She looked pale and tender, a white scarf tied round her head like a nun's coif. Before he could say "good morning" she had started to mumble an apology. As he watched her mouth moving Stagg saw the beads of sweat on her forehead.

"Not feeling so good, eh?" he said cheerily as he filled the metal basket of the espresso coffee machine.

"I haven't slept at all. Nothing but dreams, dreams. They were so violent, Malcolm. I got frightened. I forgot who I was."

Stagg cocked his head and adjusted the toaster.

"Go for a walk and clear your head," he advised. "You'll feel better by midday."

"It's the turbulence I can't stand," Joyce said faintly. "How you can be so rock-solid, I don't know." She stirred her tea then pushed it away. "Take my mind off it. What were you going to tell me last night?"

"Oh, that can wait. I have to start work."

"But it was important, wasn't it?"

Stagg cut two slices of wholemeal bread to put into the toaster. Both of them were too thick and, when crammed into the slot, broke into pieces. He switched the toaster off at the plug then turned it upside-down and shook the fragments out.

"Nothing's going right this morning," he joked. "Whenever I get up with an idea in my head and I want to put it down in as unmodified a way as possible, life conspires against it. I'm already losing my hold on the details."

Joyce stared at him.

"That's exactly what happens to me. Since I got back from Tunisia it's been terrible. Last night I lay in bed tossing and turning and I suddenly thought: 'It was a land-mine in my mind'. I was so taken with the idea that I put the light on and wrote it down in my notebook. When I looked at it this morning it said, 'Mind mine in my hand'. What does that mean?"

Stagg buttered the pieces of broken bread and spread them with ginger preserve as the coffee came through the machine with a roar.

"It will all settle down," he assured her. "We'll get back to normal soon."

"No, I don't think we will. I don't know what that means any more. Not since I came to live here. I've burned my bridges, son. Moira says I have to be careful. All my security has gone."

Stagg released his hold on the precious idea which he had been cradling in his mind since getting out of bed. It was already lost, devoured by his mother's distress. As he poured his coffee into his favourite black and gold Spanish hand-made cup, he decided to make the best of it and tell her what had been on his mind the previous night and get it out of the way.

"How would you feel about someone else coming to live with us?" he said.

"Depends on who it is."

87

"Well, it's a woman."

"Rosamund?"

"Yes, but that's not her name. Her real name is . . . "

There was a frozen pause as Stagg frantically scanned his memory for the name of the woman to whom he had made love last Friday afternoon in a basement flat behind the Whittington Hospital at Archway, London.

"Perhaps we'll just call her Rosamund for now," he eventually had to say. "I've known her for over a year."

"Do you love her?"

"Yes."

"You mean that you think you love her."

"No, I mean that I do love her."

"But you can't remember her name," Joyce sniffed, her eyes becoming more frosty. "I don't think much of that."

"Until I walked into this room and found you sitting here, I could remember it," Stagg sighed. "It's a silly name, an exotic name, the kind of name you'll sneer at."

"Do I sneer a lot, then?"

"Quite a lot."

"I thought I'd end up getting the blame."

"Well, you're a bit hard on people sometimes. They can't help what they get called, or what their basic natures are."

"That's true enough. You should hear what our Cissy says about you and what she called me. You haven't asked but I had a terrible time up there." Joyce's mouth tightened and she pronounced her anathema with an intensity of feeling which Stagg found alarming. "When I die I want you to remember that our Cissy musn't come to the funeral. I don't want her there."

"Don't feud with Cissy," Stagg advised, endeavouring to draw her out of her vindictive mood in case it should be later turned on him. "She was always a good sister to you and she was always kind to me."

"Not any more, she isn't," Joyce retorted. "She thinks you're nothing but a big head who's got above himself."

Stagg looked at his watch.

"I should be getting along," he murmured. "I think you're beginning to feel better."

"Yes, I am, but don't go for a minute."

There was a silence as Stagg made the dregs of his coffee last while he prepared himself to wind down the conversation into something trifling and purged of emotion before he left. He could see that his mother was scenting the wind of his anxiety, stalking another encounter, another argument; and this he wished to avoid.

"Don't turn against me, son," she said as he put his cup back into its big, deep saucer. "I know I'm being a nuisance to you right now and disturbing your work but I can't help it. Perhaps we should never have gone to see Frank's grave? Perhaps he was better left alone where he is?"

Stagg shook his head and laced his long, sensitive fingers together.

"Never. We had to go," he told her, ignoring his own advice to himself to steer clear of any area of conflict until later in the day when he had done his stint at the drawing-board. "No matter what happens I'll always think that it was a good thing we went."

"Moira thinks I wasn't strong enough for it."

"What does she know about how strong you are? I know. Next time she's undermining your confidence send her to see me. I'll tell her what a tough customer my mother is."

He leant over and kissed her damp cheek.

"Sometimes I wonder if I shouldn't just take it easy and give up all this agitation," Joyce mused, mollified by his display of affection. "After all, I've got all the comforts of home. I could take up gardening, do some voluntary work . . . " Stagg, on impulse, gave her a second, reinforcing kiss and squeezed her wrist.

"Whatever you decide to do is all right by me," he said. "All I want is your happiness." Then he left in a glow of good nature, feeling that he had said the right thing.

It was not until he had walked the length of his house, whistling softly to himself as he passed through oval chambers, eye-shaped halls and rib-cage fenestrated conservatories that he remembered the name of the woman with whom he had supposed himself to be in love.

89

Appalled that he could ever have planned marriage on the basis of the superficial feelings which he now recognised, he rang the woman up and broke off the affair. Mardia — for that was the name which he could not summon to his memory to compete with his mother's claims to his attention — was not at home and the message was left on her answering-machine.

Two hours later Joyce rang through on the intercom while Stagg was in his work-suite concentrating on some modifications to a super-prison for the government of Peru. It was a knotty piece of design which had made him cross as he did not believe that the alterations were necessary.

"Are you busy?" his mother asked. "I don't want to disturb you if you are."

"You've already disturbed me. I asked you to leave me alone so I could work through till lunch," Stagg replied irascibly. "What is it that can't wait?"

"I can't tell you without being face to face."

Stagg smothered a sigh and told her to come down. As he glanced at the drawing which he had been labouring over he realised that he was glad of the break. By the time Joyce appeared he had warmed to the idea of seeing her. At least she did not reek of compromise as his morning's work had done. He had spoilt a good, homogeneous design for the sake of Peruvian government economies.

"Sit down," he said, clearing a pile of drawings off a stool. "What's on your mind?"

Joyce obediently climbed on to the stool, hooking her toes behind a support-bar.

"What's that you're doing?" she asked, craning her neck to see across the drawing-table.

"It's a prison," Stagg told her, enjoying the moment of her reaction. "It's to be built in Trujillo in Peru. They're going to call it *La Prisión de las Almas*."

"What does that mean, Malcolm?" Joyce asked, her hands holding on to the edge of the seat as if she anticipated an unsettling reply.

"The Prison of the Souls." Stagg told her.

"How dare they call it that?" Joyce cried indignantly. "They're taking a lot for granted, aren't they?"

Stagg gave her a world-weary smile; his testimony to all the problems of conscience which faced him as a fee-earning architect. His mother frowned, then slowly put up one hand to fluff the curls on one side of her head and Stagg noticed, with a start, that she had dyed her hair jet black. What worried him was that it had taken until now for the change to register.

"Do you ever get worried about doing that kind of work?" Joyce said. "I was just thinking; the Nazi gas ovens must have been designed somewhere; a man with some paper and pencils who saw things in his head."

"Would you rather be an inmate in a well-designed prison or a badly-designed prison?" Stagg retorted defensively.

Joyce got down off the stool and looked over the top of the tilted drawing-table, her newly dyed hair glowing in a frizzled halo by the light of the strong lamps.

"I'm haunted by something," she declared sombrely. "I can't get it out of my mind. It's so heavy on my conscience that I can't sleep. Was that all true what you told me about school? The things they did to you?" The halo shook as if blown by a wind. "I've been brooding about it a lot lately. How could I have sent you to such a place, son?"

Stagg averted his eyes, his heart withering with shameful fear. Joyce continued to speak, telling him that she could not stop thinking about what he must have suffered, and her keen sense of guilt. While she talked, Stagg selected a fresh 2B pencil from the box and pressed the needle point along the edge of a perspex ruler until the lead broke, then started doodling to hide his feelings.

"I know you don't like thinking about it but now that you've let the cat out of the bag it's got to be settled," Joyce said. "I think I can cope with everything else but not that. As far as I can see I'm a mother who condemned her child to years of pain."

"I shouldn't have mentioned it," Stagg replied morosely, his head still lowered. "I don't know what came over me. It must have been seeing the grave, I suppose. Anyway, it wasn't years and years. Only the first two were bad."

"Two years!" Joyce cried, holding her cheeks. "To a child that's a lifetime."

"But I'm not a child any more," Stagg said, his tongue heavy. "I don't want to think about it."

"Since coming back from seeing your father's grave I'm not able to think of you in any other way than bending over."

"Don't! For heaven's sake!" Stagg said, putting his hands over his ears, "that makes me feel ridiculous. I let all that out by accident." He paused, softening his fraught expression. "Ma, listen, I don't blame you at all. I understand completely why I was sent away. It was for my own good. If I'd stayed at home I would probably have ended up in an approved school anyway."

"That doesn't say much for me, does it? What a woman! I was your mother. It was up to me to bring you up properly."

"No boy ever had a better mother," Stagg said. "It was out of your control, and anyway, look at me now. I survived."

"But I must know the truth, Malcolm. That pain is as real to me as this living minute. It's the only one I can't resolve. Do you understand? If I think that you're still hiding things from me I'll never rest. Please, tell me everything."

So Stagg gave in. In a peculiarly euphoric state of mind in which he relived the black diary of his punishments, he told his mother all he could remember. She flinched as he mustered the worst of the facts — the school record for thrashings in his second term (ninety-two strokes) — the different weapons used by the masters — the pride in not crying out or shedding tears — the ritual exposure of the crimson weals across his buttocks to the other boys in the showers. At the end of his account he was exhausted and plagued with a feeling that all would have been better left unsaid, and he put this to her.

"No, son, I'm all right now," she answered. "Now you've told me everything we can let the whole thing be forgotten. I'll never mention it again if I can help it. Thank you for going through it all again for me. Now that's out of the way we can be more natural with each other. Okay? A little lie down is in order, I think."

She made an awkward exit. Stagg's heart ached for her as he saw how heavily she walked, like an old crone. He cursed himself for his weakness in revealing the truth to her, then went back to his drawing. As he looked down at it he saw what he had been doodling and his breath went still. What the hell has got into me? he asked himself. How could I do this?

While his mother had been enduring the hoarded details of his chastisements and suffering them vicariously with him, he had sketched her into his drawing as a caryatid, a load-bearing pillar to withstand six hundred kilo-Newtons, being the anticipated down-ward thrust of five floors of concrete in the west wing of The Prison of the Souls.

Chapter Eight

Children enter your life, Joyce thought as she looked out of the eastern tower; they arrive like something which has streaked out of the sky. Who are they? Where have they come from? You give them a name. Anything you call them is meaningless. It's as silly as naming the stars. When I looked at him I thought *Malcolm*. What made me do that? I could have called him *The Destroyer*. Until he was born I had Frank in his place, dead. It was terrible but I'd managed to kill him in my mind. The whole, horrible thing — being blown apart, every pain he'd been through. But I couldn't stop his child bringing him back. At first I looked at the baby and saw the ghost.

Her bed was spread out with open books, the overspill from the desk which Malcolm had installed for her. The books went into the en suite bathroom, lying round the oval bath and toilet pedestal. There was a resistance within her to picking them up. They were stepping-stones to a new self which she was starting to distrust. What was the value of change for change's sake? What would she end up as when the whole process had finished? An absurd old woman, out of her depth, out of her time: an old age pensioner struggling to brazen out her decline and guilty dreams.

Rooks from a nearby copse flew over the tower in a noisy flock, their dark shapes ragged against the late-afternoon light. She put out a hand and picked up the first open book it encountered. It was war-time romantic fiction belonging to Mrs Hankinson which the daily help had passed on to her when she had finished it. Joyce read a few paragraphs, picking up the style, her mind tuning in. Though it dealt with all the things she had been brooding about it did not touch the core of her feelings. There was a facile, decorative device at work which provided a surface slippery with deceptions. It was gilded slop, lush with fancies, glutinous with false feelings, everything for effect, nothing tough or real. But it worked on her, resurrecting her old self and the chair she had sat in for decades, reading four or five library books a week, all of them out of the jelly-moulds of this kind of drama.

She sat up and looked at the books littered about the room. She felt a strong desire to stamp on them all. It had been a prison made of books, that fifty years. Now there had been a change and everyone was being let out — the Russians, the Germans, the Romanians, everyone — but did they know the place where they'd been? I was there, she thought, holding her hands together, and I've come out at the same time. The war was my prison but there are times when it feels like home. Whatever happens, I must never yearn to go back. And I must distinguish between books and books. She threw the novel which Mrs Harkinson had given her across the room, watching it spread its wings and crash into the wall. It's all right for you, Moira, she thought to herself, deliberately reading pulp fiction and watching bad television to stun your brain, but I can't play any more games with that kind of pollution.

"I'd like us to get to the stage where we can talk about important things without having to do it through books," Joyce announced as she walked with her son along the shore. "I must have someone who'll go through it all with me and not be ashamed."

Stagg did not ask what she meant by *ashamed*. Since leaving university thirty years ago he had felt the deprivation of one who had loved to talk earnestly on great subjects with no holds barred. He remembered whole nights of undergraduate debate but not about *self*, for the self had not accumulated by that age. The self accrued like the sand and was equally shifting; but now he had more than enough of it.

"Do you feel that you can discuss these things with me?" he asked deferentially. "If you find it difficult to do that because I'm your son, don't be afraid to say so."

Joyce moved away from him a little, putting a useful space between them.

"I've told you so many lies in the past that I don't see how you can believe anything I say," she declared, her face turned towards the sea-wind. "When you used to ask me about your father I always fobbed you off."

Stagg thrust his hands deeper into his pockets and pondered. He had no inclination to comfort his mother on this point. She, in collusion with his grandmother, whom he had adored, had kept the life of the family before the war and his birth as a veiled mystery. Within it sat his father, Frank, a soul prefigured by his death in Stagg's mind. The women had never allowed him to come to life.

"I always assumed that you had your reasons," he said eventually but with little conviction, "or that the truth was so bad that you daren't tell me."

"No, no, son," Joyce replied with a strained laugh, "it wasn't that I told you nothing at all. I made something up, a hero, a romance, you know what I mean."

Stagg nodded dismissively, then gave an audible sigh. "Oh, that," he grunted. "I never took any of that seriously."

"I did."

He looked at her, suspecting a ploy. As a woman, he had always found her honest, free of deceit. The only untruth between them was from childhood when she had not been a woman at all, but a goddess of tragedy. That had been all art to him, the art of grief, the art of a false creation. Deep down he had believed that she had known that it was the fabrication of a terrified girl facing widowhood, a child at her breast, the sky black with Hitler's bombers and Liverpool's earth splitting with flame. No wonder she had made up a fantasy of the husband who had protected her. It had been a needed lie.

"You wouldn't prefer a professional?" Stagg said with unnecessary pomposity. "A priest, for instance?"

"You know I can't stand priests," Joyce replied harshly. "They work out of a book, anyway. No, it has to be you, I'm afraid. Moira Hankinson is too shallow, though she does make me laugh. She enjoys her own problems too much to be able to think clearly about anyone else's. Isn't it terrible? At my age and here I am begging for one person who can share my thoughts?"

"Don't throw the books away," Stagg advised her. In his tone was a cagey agreement that he would do his best to give more of his time to her. Right now he wanted to talk about his loss. Mardia's beauty beckoned to his memory. He had chosen never to see her again and he could not say why without castigating his own character.

"I was a bit hasty mentioning that somebody might be coming to live with us," he mumbled, his eyes averted. "Forget all that. I was getting too far ahead of myself."

"Well, I can't say that I'm surprised that you've had second thoughts. I don't think you were all that keen on her, were you?"

"I am when I'm with her," Stagg confessed, cringing inwardly as he anticipated the acridity of her reply. He was not to be proved wrong in his prediction.

"That's shameful! This poor girl — whoever she is — would die if she knew how little you valued her," Joyce cried.

Stagg admitted that he had become shifty in love matters.

"I don't trust my feelings any more, not those feelings anyway. What are they all about?"

"They should be about children," Stagg's mother told him sternly. "I think with you it's more to do with sex, pure and simple."

Stagg's footsteps meandered a little as he thought his way through what she had said.

"You may be right," he said finally. "I do like sex but I don't like domesticity."

"There you are. Who else likes sex and doesn't like domesticity? An eighteen-year old boy. I've said to myself in the past, 'This behaviour of our Malcolm's can't go on. He's got himself too much in the wrong. Every time he finishes a building he finishes a wife.'"

"Steady on," Stagg objected. "I've finished a lot more buildings than wives."

"That's beside the point. The principle holds. You use a woman to keep your work flowing, then you ditch her." She stopped walking, directed his gaze back at Hilbre, its glittering towers thrust into the sky, hooks and gargoyles threatening from roof level. "What a place. It was never built for a woman and children to live in, son," she told him. "What it says to me is 'watch out!' I don't mind living in it now because my domestic days are over but any young woman looking at it would be put off. Except, perhaps, for an actress. Do you know any actresses?"

"Not whom I'd like to live with."

"It's a house for a woman to perform in, not live in."

"Is it?" Stagg said, hurt. "I didn't mean it to be like that."

"Yes, you did. You saw everyone fitting in like bits of furniture."

"No, I didn't . . . " Stagg protested mildly. "I thought I was giving something, not imposing."

"Better to have kids than too much of yourself."

"Is it a good time to have children?" Stagg asked. "A poisoned world, the age of greed and consumerism, the death of the mind, the end of religion . . . " He paused, aware that his lack of belief in these ideas was too obvious. His mother disliked that sort of glib claptrap and, considering her search for knowledge, it was an unfeeling game to play. He mumbled an apology and lapsed into silence.

"When I conceived you I knew that there was going to be a war," she replied after some consideration. "I knew Frank would join up and might get killed like he did. His child would make him live on, and, I must say, it was the way most women thought about it. We wanted to keep the men alive, somehow. And you're telling me that you'd rather do that with *buildings*?"

Stagg looked at the worm-casts on the sand, perfect spirals which were monuments to a dim urge to eat, breed and die. Their shapeliness made him want to be at his drawing-table facing a large, blank piece of paper on which he could improve upon life's imperfections. Once again he had lied to his mother about his fear of having children. The danger was that to have something so concrete arrive in one's life might do away with the urge to build and his creativity might dry up. As the years had gone by and his fights with womankind had multiplied and become more acrimonious, he had turned increasingly to his mother as the one female he could be close to without danger.

Stagg allowed her to walk behind him all the way to the edge of the grey sea. When he reached the water he stepped a pace into the shallows, giving her something with which to break the silence. Before she spoke and obliged him by saying that he was ruining his good shoes, he thought that he heard her struggling for breath.

"Are you all right?" he said, turning round.

Her mouth was open and she had a hand pressed against her breast.

"It's only my bronchitis," she gasped. "It comes and goes."

The next day Stagg took his mother to London for a medical examination. When it was over he had a private discussion with his doctor who submitted the facts in a straightforward way, giving Stagg no room for doubt. He was told that his mother should never catch cold because if she did the results could be fatal. However, if she kept free of all lung infections, she could live a long time. To this end the doctor advised Stagg that his mother should go to a sanitorium in Switzerland and, once brought back to health, should stay in a nursing home in a warm dry climate for the rest of her life.

"The cost will be horrendous," the doctor said finally. "So, it's up to you whether you want to keep her or not."

Stagg left the consulting rooms and took his mother out to lunch, during which he remained silent. On the drive home he began to talk.

"You don't have to go into all that," Joyce said. "My own doctor put me wise about my lungs some time ago."

"Why didn't you tell me?" Stagg protested.

"What could you do about it?"

"I could have sent you to Switzerland."

"I don't want to go to Switzerland. It's not on my list."

"Well, put it on. It will make you better."

"Listen, son, this shortness of breath will be gone by the end of the week. It has a mind of its own. Don't worry."

Stagg tried to persuade her to go for a month, at least, but she would not hear of it.

"I've taken my choices, Malcolm," she said. "I decided to come and live with you and be involved with your life. I'm not changing that just because of bronchitis. Everyone who comes from Liverpool dies from bronchitis. It's the draught from the Mersey Tunnel." She gave him a nudge with her elbow, encouraging him to smile; but he could not.

Stagg drove fast, his eyes on the corridor of light which his headlamps cut through the darkness. He had always hoped that his mother would last a long time so he would be able to give her an extra life beyond that which she had suffered. Now it was jeopardised by something as minor as a mundane, common-or-garden cold, something which swirled in every wind and skulked in every damp breath she would breathe here on the Norfolk coast where he had built his house. In his anguish he pounded the horn and the warning sound blared through the deep country night, violent, futile and sad.

Joyce's bronchitis abated, as she had promised, and her health improved. She had medication to take and this she did, obediently, letting Stagg see her swallow the pills and use the Ventolin inhaler; also she took every step to prevent catching cold, keeping out of the rain, avoiding the damp, eating plenty of fresh fruit. But when Stagg announced that he had to go to one of the dampest and most unhealthy places on earth to anyone suffering from bronchial weakness — Estonia — she said that she had to accompany him.

"Why don't you just cut your throat and be done with it?" he squawled in his bewilderment. "Estonia isn't damp, it's *dank*!"

"I want to come," Joyce told him obstinately.

"Whatever for?" he demanded. "Could it be sheer perversity?"

"Because I've got it on my list."

Stagg checked his tongue, having no real answer to this; then he pleaded with her: "Wait until I can take you somewhere warm and dry. I've got to go to California soon. That would be much better all round."

"Anyone who has watched television has been to California," she replied tersely. "I know that I wouldn't like it. It's not on my list."

Stagg lowered his head, groaning. He had been twice to Estonia, a land tucked under the armpit of Leningrad and struggling to survive all the shocks of a newly opened future. He had liked the place and had said as much to his mother. That had been his mistake.

"You're not afraid?" he asked her. "It really is a chesty place."

"Yes, I am," she replied, "and I'm not prepared to stay afraid. That's no way for anyone to live. From now on I have to go forward."

"So, you won't go to Switzerland for the good of your health but you will go to Estonia to take a risk with your health? Is that what you're saying?"

"If you like," she replied, "though that's not the way I look at it. All I want to do from now on is not waste my time."

"But how am I going to deal with it?" Stagg asked her in some distress. "I'm your son. It's my duty to look after you. How can I stand by and let you feed yourself to the undertaker."

"Oh, come off it, Malcolm," she replied with a hardening of her lips. "I'm not having you treating me like an invalid. Bronchitis isn't the end of the world. You had it enough when you were a child."

"Did I?" he asked nervously. "Was it very serious?"

"Oh, yes. I thought we were going to lose you. It was touch and go in those days before they had all these modern drugs. But, you must realise that you could become as vulnerable to bronchitis as me."

Stagg took a deep breath. He remembered how, at school, the other boys had mocked him for the little gasps he made when dressing in the morning by his bed in the dormitory. That had been over thirty-five years ago when he was thirteen and fourteen. Since then he had never had any problems with his breathing at all.

"All right," he said, trapped by their kinship of weakness, "as usual with you, it's against my better judgement, but all right. I'll take you to Estonia but don't go blaming me if it kills you."

In order to get his mother a visa Stagg had to claim that she was his technical assistant. The other architects in the project partnership which was handling the Estonian commission ribbed him about taking his mother on the trip rather than a girlfriend, but Stagg had all his answers ready. His mother was brave, he told them, and she wanted to *see*. As a companion, as a friend, and as a woman, she was worth any passing, shallow pleasure. Eyebrows had been raised. Little understanding had been shown. But it had not mattered.

They flew to Stockholm and from there to Tallinn, the Baltic seaport capital of Estonia which lies two hundred and fifty miles to the west of Leningrad. As Stagg watched his mother closely to check whether the pressurised cabin was having an ill-effect on her respiration, he told her what he knew of Estonia's history. What impressed her most was the fact that the people had only ever had twenty years of independence — the years between the two world wars — otherwise they had been ruled by foreign powers; the Danes, Swedes, Germans and Russians, for their entire history.

"Twenty years," she repeated thoughtfully, "and that's all."

"So, they're quite youthful politically as it were."

"That's when I was independent, if I ever was independent," Joyce said, "when I was a child, up until I was twenty. My father was an old tyrant but he could never get through to me. As a girl I always knew where I was going. I never had any doubt in my mind that I'd be a ballerina one day. Have I ever told you that before?"

Stagg told her that she had not but it was no surprise, considering her talent for dancing, then he proceeded to explain the background to the Soviet occupation of Estonia in 1940 after rigged elections.

"The United States never recognised Estonia as part of the Soviet Union," Stagg said. "And, to be honest, in some ways I think it never has been. The Estonians are a bit like the Jews. They are always apart, even if they do have no real autonomy to speak of."

Joyce did not write any of the information down in her notebook which lay open in her lap. Stagg was disappointed, feeling that he had failed to make it interesting enough.

Joyce found Tallinn a misty, grey, stony city wrapped in heavy black clouds; a place of high walls and towers. The cobbled square of the medieval town hall shone with an oily light, the sound of boots always rattling. From the central hill dark-noted bells boomed briefly, dolefully telling the passing hours. It was all weight, power, gloom and grimness, which she recognised. Men in uniform were everywhere, fresh-faced boys some of them, their features as varied as a netful of mixed fish. All sorts, all shapes, and everyone was waiting.

Stagg was ahead of her, about to go down a narrow alley. He had paused to examine a building which had been crammed between two high-gabled fourteenth-century houses, and his face showed the regret which he felt at the result. As she watched him, Joyce felt her breath get lighter. Within a couple of seconds she was gasping: stepping into a doorway she put a Ventolin inhaler to her mouth and pressed, tasting the chemicals as they atomised in her throat. Her breathing eased almost immediately and she sighed with relief. Stagg turned from his survey of the building and caught her with the inhaler still in her hand but she managed to palm it back into her handbag without him seeing it, then distracted his attention by pointing to a section of the city wall which carried a cone-roofed tower with arrow-slits which was reminiscent of a castle in a child's pop-up book, an image from a sinister fairy tale.

"Look at that!" she cried, her voice cracking.

Stagg loped to her side and grinned up at the tower. "Pure Walt Disney, isn't it?" he said. "We'll go in, if you like. It's an artists' hangout — the Cinematographic Club."

"Will they let us in if we're not members?" Joyce asked, buying time to settle her trembling body. "I wouldn't want to impose."

"I'm an honorary member," Stagg told her with a touch of fixer's smugness. "The government arranged it for me. Everyone wants to get in to the artists' clubs. It's the only place where there's any life."

Inside the club Stagg bought a bottle of Moldavian brandy — which was the only alcoholic drink available that day — and a brown paper bag of cashew nuts, then took Joyce to sit down at a long table in the base of the tower. Above them rose the great cylinder of stone, terminating in a timber-spoked roof. There was only a single floodlight up into the tower, and a few candles stuck in bottles on the table.

"They must be economising on the electricity," Joyce said in an undertone. "I can't see if there's anything in my glass."

Stagg smiled and scanned the faces of the other people at the table. There were six of them, all listening to a burly man in a grey trilby hat who was doing funny voices. He stopped and sat down to a flutter of applause. In the silence afterwards the man sitting next to Stagg leant over and informed him, in English, that the performer had been impersonating Leonid Brezhnev, without the help of electricity.

Stagg's embarrassment was visible as he straightened his spine and stared up into the empty space above his head. The man, who was a strongly built, Saxon-headed fellow in his early forties, patted Stagg on the shoulder and murmured that no offence had been taken.

"In Estonia we are so disparaging about ourselves that it is impossible to insult us. But," he added, "say to your wife that we keep the lighting low so all the ladies will look their best."

Stagg hastened to tell him that the woman was not his wife but his mother. The man peered over his shoulder and blamed the dimness for his error.

"If it creates that kind of mistake we must switch on all the lights," he said with a grin. "We must not induce that kind of nightmare in our guests."

Joyce had been listening, her ears ever sharp. When the stranger had finished talking she propped her face up on her elbows and looked along the table at him, a candle flame close to her cheek.

"Can you see the wrinkles now?" she asked impudently, with a shade of chagrin; then added: "I was young for my age until this year."

"So, what happened to you?" the man asked, amused.

"My son here persuaded me to come and live in his house so he could look after me. Since then I've gone downhill a lot."

Stagg joined in the laughter but he was hurt. There was enough good humour left in him, however, to cover his mother's unkind joke by working up a conversation with the man and his wife and eliciting from them their names, jobs and backgrounds. The man was the editor of a local newspaper, appointed to his senior post that very day, and he had come to the Cinematographic Club to celebrate. But he had found it hard to be cheerful, things being as they were. Then he had met Stagg and his mother and the load had lightened. Upon finding out the cause of Stagg's visit, and the fact that his mother had come on a kind of sight-seeing holiday, he said that the world seemed rosier.

"Now, at least, I have something to laugh at," he said, splashing Moldavian brandy from his bottle into his glass. "Our misery, our agony, our frightening future, is now a tourist attraction."

These words struck chords which were becoming ominous to Stagg. A gnawing, querulous sorrow had provided their impetus. He had been in a few drinking-bouts with the Estonians and, like their cousins the Finns, they occasionally sank into a poisonous gloom which made them hard company. As Stagg prepared to extricate himself and his mother from any potential trouble, the editor spoke again.

"I hope that you have not come to mock," he said, glowering. "We deserve some respect for our suffering."

"You're not the only ones who've suffered," Joyce retorted, "and if I want to come here on holiday for a bit of fun I don't see why I shouldn't."

"Take us seriously, please," the editor said with vexed, haughty politeness, straightening up in an attempt to put his shoulders on a line with Stagg's. "Be sensitive, if you can."

The editor's wife touched him on the sleeve to indicate how she thought that the confrontation had gone far enough, but her husband was in a plunging spiral of spleen and not willing to be pulled out of his descent.

"You come here," he said harshly, "knowing only what you read in the British newspapers — which are the most decadent in the world . . ."

"Oh, are they now?" Joyce rejoined, her voice plangent with animosity. "I bet they're better than Estonian newspapers any day."

"You think that you understand," the editor ground on, "but you have no idea what our problems are." He took a deep breath, shaking his head so his thinning, flaxen hair shivered on his scalp. "It is all ethnographical."

Joyce looked at Stagg, hoping for a lead: but he remained silent, unwilling to comment in case he fanned the smouldering fire of the friction between them. *Ethnographical* remained hanging in the air until the editor raised his fist and lowered it on to the table in slow motion. "A million Estonians," he intoned; then, repeating the gesture, "six hundred and fifty thousand Russians." He sat back and folded his arms. "It is a Belfast situation we have here."

Stagg's heart quailed as he saw how this remark thrust his mother deeper into her antipathy towards the editor. To her, Belfast was a shrine of holy ire, a source of atavistic wrath against all forms of political intelligence. No place on earth was like it, or had its insoluble grief.

"What do you know about Belfast?" she demanded, her blue eyes bulging with acrimony. "I'm from Belfast people. My mum and dad were Belfast, but I'm English through and through. Can't you make your mind up or something? Don't you know who you belong to?"

The editor turned to Stagg, appealing for help.

"What is she saying?"

"Ma, this has gone far enough . . . " Stagg began to remonstrate, but his mother cut him short.

"One thing I'll tell you," she rapped heatedly, finger jabbing, "there's no one place the same as the other. Am I sitting in a club in Belfast or a club in . . . " She turned to Stagg, irritated by her failure of memory. "What's this place called?"

"Tallinn," Stagg replied in a low voice.

"Yes, it is Tallinn," the editor smirked heavily. "Where did you think you were? New York?"

Joyce was lost for words. Her small lapse of memory had cost her the advantage. She subsided into a withering silence, glaring up into the cold stone cylinder above her head. The editor grunted with sour satisfaction and turned his back.

Stagg picked up the bottle of Moldavian brandy and was about to slip it into his pocket prior to making a quiet exit when Joyce leant across and tapped the editor on the shoulder. He turned, ready to sneer.

"I'm sorry, son," she said with a tough grin. "But people from Liverpool feel a lot for what goes on in Belfast. We're the same in many ways. All in one frying pan."

The editor nodded, accepting Joyce's apology with an initial churlishness which lightened as he saw the expression on her face and understood the effort which she was making.

"I should not be arguing with you," he said. "Lady from Liverpool, find it in your heart to forgive me. If I may explain; what has upset me is the presence of this animal." He pointed down the table to a bowed figure with bald head and glasses. "He used to have my job. When he was editor he encouraged the Russians to come and settle here. If anyone can be blamed for making Estonia into Ulster, it is men like him."

Joyce sipped at her brandy. She could see the glint of the accused man's eyes behind his wire spectacles and the movement of his fingers round the stem of his glass.

"He's a collaborator," the editor growled, "a Soviet stooge. I have to sit in his chair at work and it makes me sick."

The man at the end of the table raised his head and spoke in what Joyce assumed was the Estonian language. He was extremely drunk, slurring his words and swaying on his seat, but she thought that he managed to convey some kind of dignified opposition.

"What's he saying?" Joyce asked the editor.

"Nothing. Not even communist rhetoric these days. He's just

complaining," came the rancid reply. "He should go into a wood and hang himself so we don't have to look at him."

His soul affronted by this remark, Stagg got sharply to his feet and virtually commanded his mother to return with him to the hotel: " . . . for dinner," he added as an afterthought which she could use as leverage to break the dialogue.

"I don't want any dinner. I'd rather stay here," Joyce replied. "Does that man at the end speak English?"

"No!" roared the editor. "He can only speak RUSSIAN!"

There was a tinkle of breaking glass as the compromiser slumped forward with his face in his arms. The other people around the table gave him the briefest of contemptuous glances then resumed their own conversations.

Stagg remained on his feet, feeling very tall as he looked down from the gloom on to the candle-lit table. He knew that his mother would come now, the act having come to its natural close.

Over dinner that night the matter was not mentioned but Stagg could see that his mother was struggling to think her way through it all and disconsolation would be her only reward.

"Don't let that scene in the club upset you," he said as they drank coffee. "Everything is very small scale here. You can't escape from the problems. They hit you straight away."

Joyce shrugged and held a cube of sugar in her coffee so it absorbed the brown liquid, then popped it into her mouth.

"You did warn me," she murmured as she crunched the sugar cube, "but you know your mother, son. She's never taken enough notice of what people say."

Chapter Nine

Stagg had breakfast early and left for a meeting with officials of the government department of the Marine. As Tallinn is a small, well-defined city, he had no apprehension in leaving Joyce to her own devices for the morning, having provided her with a street map and some currency. She was not up by the time he left the hotel so he scribbled a note at the desk to say that he would ring at eleven o'clock to make further arrangements to meet up with her once his meeting was over.

The old, black, well-maintained government car rumbled through the back streets below the citadel, the smell of its worn leather a pleasure in his nostrils. He was glad to have reached the stage with his mother whereby he could, with equanimity, leave her to fend for herself in a strange city. Before Hilbre had been built and the responding change in Joyce had taken place, he would never have been able to do this. Now, even though she was so much more vulnerable, he knew that her strength had been made greater. No matter what problems she faced in the ancient capital of the Estonians, she would be able to deal with them.

The driver nursed the car over a cobbled surface, brushing the flying coats of the passers-by as they crowded the narrow street in a funnel of wind. Stagg watched the headscarved women, knowing that in the eighteen months during which he had been making visits to Tallinn he had not seen the lot of the wives get any better. They still went out every day to stand in queues for hours, patiently collecting goods, scouring the shops, wandering in and out of the stores like sheep searching for grass on a bald mountain. It was a daily motion of the city's life which both depressed and excited him, for it had a rhythm which he felt was very old. Already, in his mind, he was injecting that sense of the timeless quest for goods into his concept for the design of a shopping mall on the outskirts of Madrid. It had a brutal sweep to it, a Visigothic thrust which was paralleled here in the streets of Tallinn. In his heart he knew that it was the curve of hunger that he would be drawing, and the shape of teeth.

The steward at the Cinematographic Club recognised Joyce from her visit the previous day and did not demand proof of membership. She bought a bottle of Moldavian brandy and a brown paper bag of cashew nuts and went into the tower. The compromiser was already sat there in the light of a floodlamp in the roof, his face gaunt in the shadows which it cast from above. Joyce was glad to see that there was no one else in the place.

"I know you can speak English," she said as she sat down beside him. "I was watching you yesterday."

The compromiser looked dully at Joyce. He noticed her wedding-ring first, thin with wearing, loose and hanging on her finger. From there he examined the rest of her, wondering what she had looked like before she had lost all the weight. It was a strong face, set with lines which were graven as if in a monument, but the protruberant eyes were very open and clear. He could see no aggression except in the line of the mouth which had a firmness he feared.

"Go away," he said.

"No."

"You should."

"Who says?"

"I'm not good company," the compromiser said morosely, "and my life isn't a public performance."

"Do you sit here every day and get drunk?"

"If I do, so what?"

Joyce pushed the bottle of Moldavian brandy across to him. "You can have this," she said. "I only bought it because I thought you were expected to."

The compromiser smiled tightly, stroking his nose. Joyce saw that he had shaved that morning. He had a clean shirt on and his finger nails had been looked after.

"It's too early. I have a rule," the compromiser said as he stared at the coloured label which displayed a bucolic scene of mountains, woods and brightly costumed peasants dancing. "When ten o'clock comes, then I start drinking."

Joyce noticed the man's eyebrows which were long, thin and arched; far too elaborate for his grey eyes. It was the face of a docker, she decided, maybe a warehouse captain. Someone who might be found in the streets of Liverpool.

"My name's Joyce Stagg," she said, putting out her hand. "What's yours?"

He laughed, taking her hand and lightly touching his forehead against the label of the bottle.

"Arvo," he replied. "I think it's ten o'clock by someone's clock, somewhere."

Joyce sat with him in the tower while he drank from the bottle of Moldavian brandy. The club filled up; people came to sit at the table. None of them spoke to Arvo although they took interest in Joyce once they heard her speaking English, but she refused to give them any of her attention, her mind locked on to the story which was being told to her.

Arvo provided a fractured, ironic account of his days in the editorship of a local newspaper which had some claim to have both a popular and intellectual appeal. He had been a loyal member of the Estonian Communist Party from youth, had gone to Tartu State University where he had studied philology, and had worked his way up through the ranks of Estonian-language journalism. It had always been his opinion that Estonia could not survive as an independent political unit and, he claimed with an arrogant stare at the rest of the people around the table, he had yet to be proved wrong.

"What I did not prophesy was that my country, which I love, would not be able to survive as a member of the Soviet Union either," he said with a throaty chuckle. "But the damage was done. I had made my views well known. So, Joyce, I have had my day.

My choices were taken and I stand by them. For me, it did not work out. These people spit on me, but I don't care."

"Did you make a lot of money being an editor?" she asked.

"Ha-ha!"

"Why I'm asking is this: did you make yourself believe in something so you could get rich?"

Arvo stood up, corked the bottle of Moldavian brandy, and slipped it into his coat pocket.

"Come with me," he commanded.

"Where are we going?"

"I want you to see where I live, then you'll know how rich I became."

Joyce demurred, sparing a thought for her son who might doubt the wisdom of such a visit. Although this persecuted and unfortunate man, Arvo, pulled at her heart-strings, he was still a drunk, and a stranger.

"I'll take your word for what it's like," she said. "Describe it to me."

"Ah, you're worried about your honour!" Arvo exclaimed, hitting his forehead with the heel of his hand. "I should have thought about that. Joyce, my dear, I am a wreck. If a man has scorn and hatred heaped upon his head for a few years it affects his virility. You have nothing to fear from me."

Joyce stood up, her cheeks burning. Everyone around the table was staring at her. Some were laughing openly.

"I'm not afraid for that reason," she retorted proudly. "To be frank, I think I'm probably stronger than you are anyway."

Arvo nodded with approval and held out his arm. "Then you'll come?" he said with a lift of his chin. "I'd be delighted."

Joyce's inner resolution was tested when Arvo took her to a taxi rank where they had to stand for twenty minutes. Vehicles came and went in a bewilderingly inconsistent relationship with the queue, people from behind jumping to the front.

"This is the new capitalism," Arvo spelled out for her. "Private enterprise. The taxis all have different prices and you must know which ones you can negotiate with, or they'll rob you."

"Couldn't we take a tram?" Joyce asked, looking longingly at the old streetcars passing. "I'd love to go on a tram again. We used to have them in Liverpool."

"The trams don't go where I live," Arvo replied. "You see, Joyce, my home is in the future, not the past."

A taxi known to Arvo eventually turned up and they were driven out of the city to the north, glimpsing the Baltic as it lay in a grey slate of calm beside the black coast. Joyce looked at the silver birch trees and the houses tucked away in the woods, hoping that he would live in such a place. But the taxi went on and on.

"This drive is my only pleasure, apart from my friend," Arvo said, patting the bottle in his pocket. "I spend all my money on taxis."

The tops of high buildings began to appear above the trees. As the taxi came out into open country, Joyce saw a great plain with hundreds of tower blocks standing like the gravestones of giant warriors. There were no trees, no fields, no gardens, only the shadows of the structures falling over the cleared ground. As she looked at this desolation she found herself contrasting it with Madjez-el-Bab and its geraniums.

"You live in that?" she asked.

"That's what I'm told," he replied, a sour smile. "Is it living?"

"It doesn't seem to end anywhere."

"No, it has no real end. But it is the right place for me, as an old communist, to spend my last days. I can pick over the debris."

Joyce saw no shops, no signs of life. As the taxi zigzagged between the huge, peeling edifices, sliding in and out of their cold shadows like a snake seeking escape from a freezing maze, she saw no one, not a child on a bicycle, not a woman with a basket.

"More people live here than in the city," Arvo told her. "We thought that they'd be happier. I came to live here by choice. Isn't that wonderful? I had an old apartment near the Mound but I gave it up to join the great experiment in living on the moon."

"What were you all thinking of?" Joyce burst out. "If you looked at the design for this on a piece of paper you'd know it was inhuman. Who imagined that people could live like this?"

"People *do* live like this," Arvo responded. "They have done for years now, many long years."

"But why?" she persisted.

"It was the war," Arvo replied.

The taxi drew up at the foot of a tower block in the thick of the endless army. While Arvo paid the driver, Joyce walked to the entrance and saw the graffiti over the walls. Her heart turned as she recognised the black scream behind the insane loops and squiggles. The childish scrawl was the same as in Liverpool, a little literary dynamite which might bring the aloof bastions of authority crashing down.

"Beautiful, eh?" Arvo whispered as he ushered her into the concrete foyer which stank of urine. "As you can see, Leonardo da Vinci has been hard at work on our walls."

"I mustn't bring my son out here," Joyce said tremulously, very close to tears. "He'd go mad."

"Well, we go mad. Why should he be protected?"

"He's an architect," Joyce explained, "and he's very sensitive about buildings."

"Then he must come out to Moon City, to the Infernal Polis where the guilty are punished. Joyce, this is architectural Siberia. I feel happy here. My sins are all around me."

Arvo lived on the twelfth floor and the lift was not working. He insisted that she take a breather at every stage, pointing out the desolation from the grimy windows at each level.

"The thinking is this," he expounded, "take away all natural features and the mind of the citizen will concentrate upon the glories of scientific socialism instead. Who needs any sign of the seasons? What political advantage is there in spring or summer? You see how coherently we argued? If we could have undermined the appeal of nature, we would have won the contest."

"Why is there no one about?" Joyce panted. "I can't hear a thing?"

"Millions of roubles went in soundproofing. The whole of the Soviet Union was soundproofed so people couldn't hear each other screaming. But don't worry, they're in there, thinking away about the new Estonia and how soon they can be let out of these pigeon-lofts."

With a flourish he inserted his key into the lock of a damaged door and pushed it open. A torrent of frenetic rock music poured out into the stair-well, stopping Joyce in her tracks.

"My sons," Arvo shouted down to her. "They're saying welcome."

There were four youths in the small apartment. They had set up amplifiers and electric guitars in the sitting-room but the cables ran from every socket available. Joyce's eyes went from face to face, from hair style to hair style, in a blaze of recognition. They were the replication of the worrying visions which had stalked West Kirby and Liverpool, dyed, painted and tattooed tribal ghosts which had risen from the suffering earth, the children of the television and prating school who had become bloodily embittered by the absence of war when they had grown to warriorhood. It was the same frenzy, the same cry for the unfought conflict.

"We are forbidden to do this," Arvo said with a rueful smile as he traced out the tangle of cables with his finger. "I have been warned many times, but my sons must have their music. They will play for you, no doubt."

"They don't have to," she replied, "I've heard what they can do when they put their minds to it."

"I baptised the group. For a few months they had no name. Every name they came up with was either too ludicrous or simply stupid. Then, in 1988 I began to work out what was happening in Europe." Arvo let his words sink in, watching her with a limpid glee as she struggled to make the jump. "People were on the move. They were dissatisfied. Better pastures, more goods, more things. I suddenly saw a vision. All these political changes were from an ancient urge — the same nomadic thrust as that of the barbarian tribes in the Dark Ages. You scour the land, or the system in our case, clean, then move on. So we called the band The Slavic Scourge."

The youths shouted and stamped, shaking their hair, repeating the name and laughing with mock barbaric ferocity.

"You see? We understand each other. I sleep in one corner of a bedroom which often has a card-school in it, or a few of these boys smoking cannabis; it's crowded, but at least they speak to me — well, grunt at me. It's home. Even if I invite you into my bedroom we'll never be alone."

Joyce sat down on a battered and stained rayon-covered settee next to a bulky junction-box which had been made out of a tin.

"Do they have a job, any of them?"

"My sons? Who will give them a job? Isn't it amazing that they talk to me at all?"

Joyce looked at the bookshelf which ran along one wall. It was the place of business in the apartment, with a telephone and numbers scribed on the wall and stacks of yellowing newspapers tied with string.

"Did you write those?" she asked, pointing at the newspapers.

"Yes, they are my issues, what's left of them. My sons threw some of them out of the window when they were feeling more disrespectful than usual, but I have a few left. My editorials were much admired in their day. It was said that they had *penetration*."

The youths suddenly left the apartment in a rush, leaving all their equipment hooked up and turned on. Arvo quickly closed the door and went through the four rooms switching the power off at the wall sockets. When he had finished he went into the tiny kitchen and washed out two plastic glasses. Joyce followed him in and stood to one side, appalled at the filth but resisting the urge to roll up her sleeves and clean the place from top to bottom.

"Well, Joyce, now you have seen the penalty I pay for ideology, I think," Arvo said with a lethal smirk, "but I do have the big advantage of living in a perfect instrument of suicide."

"It's cruel. They should all be pulled down, these places," Joyce said, shuddering as she saw the condition of the drying-up towel he was using. "I hate your home."

"Thank you."

"Where's your wife?"

"She was taken away by the secret police."

Joyce scrutinised his face carefully.

"Honestly?" she said. "Is that the truth?"

"No, it is an Estonian euphemism. When a wife or a husband runs away it is blamed on the authorities. Why not? It's government which makes life unbearable, isn't it?" He paused and grinned wickedly. "We don't like to be rejected, do we? Oh Joyce, I see my wife in the arms of a new kind of compromiser. He makes deals with his conscience and he calls it democracy. That man has no vision, no dream. I feel sorry for him. How he will produce a decent newspaper, I don't know."

"Was that your wife who was with the man in the club?" Joyce asked, her voice high with incredulity.

"Who else?" Arvo replied. "Why d'you think he showed off so much?"

"But she's too young to be the mother of your sons, surely?" Joyce insisted, her mind grabbing at inconsistencies in order to avoid the full implications of what had happened in the Cinematographic Club the previous day.

"She is my second wife. My first wife left me for another communist like myself, which is to her credit," Arvo explained with a straight face, "and she was generous enough to leave behind all our children."

"And your second wife sat there yesterday and heard what that man was saying about you?" Joyce said, remonstrating with the memory in her head. "How could she do such a thing?"

"Dislike!"

"What had you done to her?"

Arvo pinched his nostrils thoughtfully, part of his conversational semaphore which Joyce had come to recognise as a signal that he was about to make a concession to non-ironic seriousness.

"That is a complex question to ask anyone, but I think I can answer it," he said with pained wistfulness. "She began to understand the way my mind worked. Before that she was an excellent wife, and stepmother to my four boys. I used to think that I was the most fortunate man in Estonia. But then . . . " he raised a finger, "she saw through me. I became transparent."

"What did she see?" Joyce asked, her eyes running over the

cartons and tins in an open cupboard and noticing a pile of crushed brown paper bags which seemed to contain very little.

"Oh, she was very clear about that," Arvo replied. "The woman is intelligent, I assure you. She said that I had talked myself into a position where the car was driving the driver."

Joyce poked a few of the brown paper bags to feel their contents. Rice, she guessed, or barley. Pasta perhaps. Flour. She knew that Arvo's eyes were on her, waiting to see if she had grasped the meaning behind his wife's metaphor.

"You should clean out this cupboard or the mice will come in," Joyce said, wiping her fingertip on the surface of the greasy draining-board. "I think I understand what she was getting at but I don't think it's a reason for leaving you in a mess like this."

They took the glasses to the settee and sat looking out of the window over the gaunt, bleak scene, the Moldavian brandy soothing their raw feelings. Now and again he turned to her and grinned regretfully but did not speak. Clouds gathered behind the tower blocks to the west and rolled in, low and thick.

"The Slavic Scourge will not be back for a few hours," he said after a while. "Beneath your innocence and severity you're a charming woman. The bedroom is in such a filthy state that I could not offer it to the mother of a sensitive British architect, so how do you feel about the floor?"

"I thought you said that you were finished?" Joyce answered pertly but with her heart racing.

"I am, but the dead can live again. Isn't that the message of Christianity?"

Joyce shook her head and stood up, going to the window.

"Not me, Arvo," she said in a voice which mingled the sardonic and the sympathetic. "I've had enough of men in bits."

He gave a muffled laugh, getting to his feet and joining her at the window. With a straightforward movement he took her hand.

"Then I'll revert to my daily routine and we'll go back to the club where I can get drunk under the noses of my fellow-Estonians who need me." He waited for her to query this point, which she failed to do. "I'm a scapegoat, taking the blame and guilt for everyone else out there." He squeezed her hand then released it but she held on, looking into his face with a questioning encouragement.

"Then that's a kind of noble sacrifice, isn't it?" she said.

Arvo grimaced as he saw that he had not broken through the walls of her simplicity. Each irony had merely been absorbed, shells shot into a hillside.

"I have a personal question to ask about the quality of your mind," he said gravely, putting her fingers to his lips. "Do you think that you have a natural curiosity?"

"Oh, I hope so," Joyce replied, taking her hand away. "I'm basing my whole future on it."

"A word of advice, then," he admonished her. "Don't ever believe that the answers are any less complicated than yourself."

"Oh, I'd never do that," Joyce averred stoutly. "I know that life's not straightforward."

"And always give respect to dreams when they're dying," he said with a melancholy laugh, pointing out of the window, "even when they're as ugly as that."

Chapter Ten

Stagg had lost his mother. He had kept calm during the day as each of his telephone calls to the hotel failed to contact her. By the time that his meetings were over it was six o'clock and she had still not returned to her room. On the way back to the hotel Stagg told the driver to call in at the Cinematographic Club to see if she was there. The steward said that Joyce had been in twice during the day, once in the morning and once in the late afternoon. She had recently left with Arvo, having been involved in a rowdy argument in the tower during which Arvo had been abused and insulted by other members. Stagg discovered that Joyce had not been drunk but very upset and had virtually carried Arvo out of the club. The steward remembered Arvo shouting that he must lie down somewhere.

Stagg returned to the hotel and ran up the stairs. As he went past the desk he caught the odd glances from the receptionist and clerk, however he did not give them a chance to halt him. He had already imagined the diplomatic nightmare whereby Joyce had entered the foyer carrying a drunken Stalinist ex-editor and dragged the reprobate up to her room, brushing aside the protests of the staff who all knew the role of this notorious figure in Tallinn's immediate political past.

He rang Joyce's room and confirmed the truth of his evil dream.

"Joyce," he said with as much patience as he could dredge up after a day of hard negotiations. "I doubt if it will endear me to the Estonians if they find out that my technical assistant has been hitting it off with a Soviet stooge."

"I can't talk now," she replied, "he's flat out and I don't want to wake him."

"Then come to my room," he pleaded. "I've got to sort this out."

"No, he's got difficulties with his breathing. He's an asthmatic. I have to keep giving him a go with my inhaler. It's a good job I haven't had to use it lately and there's plenty left."

"You shouldn't have done this to me," Stagg moaned. "This is a town full of rumours. Everyone will know what's happened by the morning. I'll lose this contract."

There was a silence at the other end of the line then she spoke tersely. "Well, don't just keep nagging at me, Malcolm. Come and see what I'm dealing with."

"No, you come here. I don't want him listening in."

"Oh, all right. You're such an old woman sometimes."

Stagg was shocked when she entered his room. Her eyes were hollow and reddened and there was dried vomit on her skirt.

"What are you playing at?" he wailed, taking her hand and sitting her down on the bed. "I thought that you'd be able to look after yourself and you immediately get into a mess like this."

"I don't like to see someone kicked when they're down," she answered him with a fiercely righteous glare. "And nor should you!"

"That's when they do kick them in politics," Stagg rejoined. "And he asks for it, doesn't he? He drowns his sorrows in public, almost begging them to have a go at him. If he had any sense he'd stay at home."

"You haven't seen his home."

"You haven't been there as well?" Stagg cried out in dismay. "What's got into you? Are you out of control?"

Joyce stood up and looked in the mirror, straightening her hair. She noticed the dried vomit on her skirt and wrinkled up her nose.

"He's killing himself. Another six months and he'll be dead, he reckons," she said gloomily. "Why can't they change the system without killing people?"

"I'm going to order a taxi to take him home. This business will cost me a fortune in tips for the hotel staff to keep quiet. Also, I'll have to let people know that you were only trying to help the man, not raping him."

Joyce went into the bathroom and started to clean her skirt with a tissue. Stagg stood in the doorway, watching her, his heart softening.

"He was part of a very repressive regime that killed thousands, sent them to labour camps, all that," he said gently. "You can't just forget recent history. He's probably lucky not to have been lynched."

"But that's all over, like the war's all over. Now he's just a survivor. What about all these other Estonians? What were they doing? Fighting in the streets? I'd never heard of Estonia till now so they must have kept pretty quiet," she snarled. "He needs a chance, poor bugger!"

The fury of her riposte took him aback. He saw that she had been touched in a bleeding wound, somewhere very sore. Withdrawing from the bathroom he went back and sat on the bed, waiting for her to come out. When she did so he saw, with approval, that her eyes were brighter and she seemed less exhausted.

"I might marry him," she announced.

"Great," Stagg sniffed, looking up from a drawing which he had spread over the pillow. "I can't think of a better father for me at my age. At least we can have some polarised discussions."

"He's asked me."

"Was he sober?"

"He's never properly sober. There's always alcohol in his blood stream. He went to the clinic one morning for some test or other and they told him that he had the equivalent of half a bottle of vodka left in him from the previous night."

Stagg put his hand on the telephone.

"Let me ring for a taxi and the porters can carry him down. He can't stay in your room."

"Then get him a room of his own for the night," Joyce suggested but with a firmness which brooked no argument. However, Stagg had to admit that it was a reasonable way out of the impasse.

"I'll go and talk to the manager," he said, folding up his drawing, "but don't be surprised if they refuse."

He left the room. After an hour's pleading and arguing in the manager's office he obtained a reluctant permission from the unnerved and outraged incumbent that Arvo could stay one night but must not use the dining-room; also, he had to be out of the hotel by first light.

Joyce made it clear that she had nothing but scorn for the hotel's concern for its reputation. She declared that if Arvo wasn't good enough to eat in the dining-room then neither was she. So dinner was ordered for Stagg's room and when it was brought Joyce made Stagg help her to carry it down the corridor to hers and they ate on either side of the sleeping Arvo before waking him up long enough to be carried to his own place of rest.

Stagg asked for an alarm call at six in the morning so he could wake Arvo and be sure that he left the hotel, as agreed. When he made the call there was no answer. Stagg got up and went to Arvo's room and banged on the door but raised no response. When he went down to the hotel desk to get a key he was informed that the compromiser had slipped away during the night.

Stagg had a silent breakfast with his mother, then left for another meeting. He returned within half an hour, grim-faced and tense, and told Joyce that because of an unforseen shift in the political situation their visit had been cut short.

The Estonian dock and harbour rehabilitation project was a big, profitable contract worth 1.5 million pounds over three years. When it was lost, Stagg had to regroup his professional interests and change his principal associates. Old and valued friends shied away from him under mildly litiginous circumstances, and Stagg discovered, to his cost in pay-offs and settlements, how boon companions can distinguish between business and loyalty when it comes to the loss of money. Stagg was dropped socially and many of his professional contacts withered because he had fouled up an important, major contract by infantile ineptitude. He was painted as an overgrown schoolboy with a mother-fixation, someone unfitted and ill-equipped to administer his own talent.

Stagg's repugnance to the treatment given him by his friends was profound, as was his disgust for the pettiness exhibited by his profession. He detected a tendency to crow over his humiliation, to be quietly satisfied with his fall from grace. Many of his competitors had cause to envy his reputation and those he could forgive; but he could not extend that to those whom he had numbered amongst his loyal colleagues. The result of his isolation was a trimming-down of his network of consultancies and directorships and a heavier concentration upon his own work.

He did not tell Joyce about these disappointments and adjustments because he felt that she should not take responsibility for them. He had fallen into the maw of that great macerator, self-righteousness, and it was the Estonian government which had failed in its duty to understand the weaknesses harboured within human compassion. The financial problems which came in the wake of the shrivelling of his business, he kept away from her, but the spectre of debt began to haunt his working-class mind. When Joyce observed his economies as they were introduced, one by one so as not to arouse her suspicions, she assumed that they were only signs that her son was coming to his senses. She had always disapproved of showy displays of wealth even though, apart from the building of Hilbre, his were quite modest in character.

In the months of late summer and early autumn, when his ostracisation was at its most acute and he was most sensitive about it, letters began to arrive for Joyce from Estonia. There had previously been correspondence from Tunisia, two aerogrammes, the contents of which she had not shared with him. Stagg's mood at this time had become cynical. He was recovering from the spitefulness of his one-time friends, the loss of Mardia's body, and struggling with the Inland Revenue. Life, he had decided was an existential frolic, not to be taken seriously. When he looked at it from the mountain-top of his aggrieved misery it all appeared to be inconsequential. On a few occasions he shared this self-pitying scepticism with Joyce who took little notice but he caught her in a susceptible moment one afternoon.

"What's the matter with you these days?" she demanded. "You never stop moaning."

This response jolted Stagg out of his melancholy and he immediately cast about in his mind for a new direction in which to take their conversation, his own unhappiness boring him as much as her. But he could not find a way out of the trap of self-indulgence and soon he heard himself moaning again, this time about taxation and the valuable time that he had to waste on accounts.

"I could do those for you," Joyce said. "Why you waste your time on that kind of thing I don't know. I spent most of my life doing sums for other people, why not you?"

Stagg shook his head. He told her that his financial affairs were extremely complicated, requiring the attention of expert account-ants and tax advisers. The part which he had to do was supply information and keep track of income and expenditure, but even that was an onerous task. The greatest bugbear of his life was the administration of the VAT which he passionately hated because it made him into a tax-collector for the government.

This interested Joyce. To be a tax-collector rather than a tax-payer was a provocative thought. She begged Stagg to allow her to do a trial run.

"But why?" he protested.

"To change the way I look at the power which is over me," she replied. "What I'm thinking about these days, Malcolm, is the nature of government. Why do we allow such authority over our lives when we have so little time and such a limited amount of energy."

"And doing my VAT accounts will help you?"

"Arvo says that it's best to work out your political thinking through practical experience. If you don't feel the brunt of power then you can't tackle it mentally."

"Is this what he told you in Tallinn?" Stagg asked, already fearing that her reply would merely confirm that a relationship was persisting.

"Not really," Joyce said with a smile which had some secretive shyness in it, "he put a lot about it in his last letter. We're pen-pals."

"Are you, now?" Stagg breathed. "I see."

"It wouldn't take much to steer Ali and Yasouf away from going on about Islam and switch their focus to proper political science. You can't have a real dialectic about the state if religion's still a force, can you?"

"Of course not," Stagg replied.

"As I said in my last letter to them — how does being a bureaucrat square up with Islam?"

"How indeed."

"Is bureaucracy central to your theology, I said."

"I'd like to see their reply," Stagg murmured. "And another big advantage is that in their daily work they have a lot to do with VAT. You can compare notes, perhaps send them photocopies of my accounts?"

"Do immigration officers have anything to do with VAT?" Joyce enquired. "They've never mentioned it."

Stagg admitted that he had made a mistake. For some reason he had confused the Tunisians with his great-uncle, who had been a customs officer. It was Her Majesty's Customs and Excise which had the responsibility for the infamous tax. As he spoke he began to laugh, then found himself weeping.

"Why are you crying, son?" Joyce asked concernedly, taking a handkerchief out of her sleeve and giving it to him.

"Oh, let's say it's just overwork," Stagg snorted, wiping his eyes, "or hay fever. You just continue your dialectic with Arvo and I'll try to cook up some scheme whereby we can provide a different way for you to feel the brunt of arbitrary power than doing my boring VAT."

"Arvo thinks I should join the British Communist Party."

"Is there one any more?"

"What are your political opinions, Malcolm? You've never told me anything about them for some reason."

Stagg suddenly knew that he had no right to deny this woman anything of his mind. To be in the last tenth of her existence on earth when most people begin to mentally prepare themselves to become a sort of humus, then bravely square up to Marx and

Aristotle, was magnificent. She would get nowhere, of course. It would all be a farce. When it was all over she would slide into the salty cynicism about politics which Stagg had been drowning in for many years. But now, in her eagerness and enthusiasm, she had to be challenged and duelled with, or Arvo and the Tunisians would have everything their own tatty and disreputable way.

"Have you got a few days?" he said with a penitential grin. "I'll tell you what I think."

"No games. I have to be serious. All my life I've voted, son. It's been a duty. But I can't remember anything about it. Arvo says that's because I'm a typical example of western decadence. I vote on prices. Look at Northern Ireland, he says, naked imperialism . . ."

"All right, all right," Stagg said, cutting her off. "Never mind what Arvo says. You asked me what I thought."

Joyce sat back and nodded, folded her hands in her lap and closed her eyes while he told her.

> Hilbre,
> Chidham,
> Nr Great Yarmouth,
> Norfolk,
> England.
>
> 10th September 1990

Dear Arvo,

　　　　Thank you for your last letter which I found quite useful as a beginning on Malcolm. As far as politics go you've no idea what the Tories stand for, that's clear. There are times when I would gladly see all the upper classes liquidised in this country, but such an attitude is all emotion. After all, they're only people, as you say, and inherited wealth is the height of unfairness perhaps, but I notice that working-class people are proud as peacocks about money. It's a shame that we still have a royal family and an aristocracy in Britain, and that rich people have all the power through corrupt influence, yet it seems to me that it has proved to be a better system, or lack of it, than communism, which never improves with age. I was only saying to my son, Malcolm, the other day, how I feel ashamed that our country is so old-fashioned about what people are worth, but the prejudice is so obvious that it seems to act as a buffer against extremism. As Malcolm says, what can you do but laugh? What kind of people want to be politicians or policemen? The first thing about them is that their instincts aren't to be trusted, and that must have been your problem when you were a big banana. You must come over and see our system yourself. I will pay for your ticket at this end and you can give me the money back when it comes to hand. Why don't you come for Christmas? I've already invited a couple of friends of mine from North Africa. They're Muslims but they venerate the Virgin Mary, the Archangel Gabriel and a few other Christian figures who overlap with their own religion.

I asked Malcolm about his next trip to Estonia but he said that the building of the new port complex is being delayed and he doesn't think it will be necessary for him to go over for a while. If we do manage another visit I'd like to see some of the other places in Estonia and look at the countryside.

Look after yourself and try to control your drinking.

Yours sincerely,
Joyce.

Arvo's reply to this letter was mordant and corrosively long, eating into Joyce's optimism with every phrase. He had written it during a bout of acute alcoholic depression when everything in his sad world was falling apart. His sons had been caught with drugs. The authorities had given him notice to quit his apartment. The committee of the Cinematographic Club had banned him from the premises. The validity of his pension was being questioned. When he looked into the future he saw nothing but more misery and final despair. The tone of Joyce's communication had irritated him well beyond the point where he could throw away the letter and forget about her. The woman had never known real loss as he had — the collapse of an entire world — and her mind was as small as any housewife's. As a philosophic friend it was his responsibility to reveal the true nature of human life to her in all its futility. Before he had posted his reply there had been a moment of doubt as he imagined the effect it would have on such a political innocent but he overcame it with a surge of destructive bad temper. Let her suffer, was his decision. It will do her good.

Joyce read it in Stagg's presence as they sat together over the VAT return. They had reached the point where Joyce had abandoned her intention to become involved in this aspect of the running of his business because it was too mundane. As Stagg shuffled the scraps of paper and credit card receipts into date order and complained about the negative effect this regurgitation of old meals and expenses had upon his artistic spirit, Joyce read the fourteen pages of closely written text, her blood running colder and colder with each line. When she had finished her face was pale.

"Have you ever thought about killing yourself?" she asked Stagg who had just reached the end of his addition of what tax he had obediently screwed out of his fellow-citizens for the British government.

"No," he replied. "I haven't, but I've never rejected the possibility, and sometimes I think that being dead must be restful."

"Why didn't you tell me?"

He looked at her. She was standing in the light of the window and he noticed, for the first time, how drawn she had become.

"Why should I?" he said. "It wouldn't be fair."

"I'm your mother. I gave you your life. If it becomes worthless then I've got a right to be told."

Stagg scowled, bundling up the row of flimsy receipts which, to a giant computer in Southend-on-Sea, was all that mattered of his life.

"What you gave me will always remain valuable," he said, "but I may not retain the wit to use it properly. If I destroyed myself it would not be a criticism of you in any way."

Joyce was quiet for a while. When she walked out of his office Stagg saw how bowed she had become as if she were carrying all the cares of the world on her shoulders.

"You taught me all you could," he called after her.

"I taught you nothing, son," she responded dejectedly. "How could I? I never knew anything."

Concerned at the obvious seriousness of her self-criticism, Stagg followed her into the kitchen where she began preparing a pot of tea, her body moving in a morose somnambulance which was punctuated by small inarticulate murmurs.

"Who was the letter from?" Stagg asked, sitting down at the long kitchen table. "Anyone I know?"

"No one you know, or I know," Joyce asserted with a brief anger, then, subsiding into despondency again, "I'd have been better off living with my ignorance. At least I'd got used to it."

"What's made you so fed up?"

In response to his question Joyce held up the letter and indicated that he should read it.

"Are you sure?" he said, crinkling his forehead. "If it's private perhaps I shouldn't?"

"It's mostly about you, son," Joyce replied, handing the letter over, "so why shouldn't you see it?"

Stagg put the letter down on the table and read it through, page by page, without stopping. Arvo had a clear, simple style in English; some jargon crept in but not too obtrusively, and he followed his arguments through with a luculent logic. The import of his main theme was a reply to Joyce's earlier letters in which she had asked him to analyse some of her problems. The one which had been causing her most trouble was her guilt over her son's maltreatment at school forty years ago. With trenchant sarcasm not far below the surface, Arvo had sketched out a socio-psychological scenario in which a traumatised pater-orphan who had reached a level of aggression beyond control, was sent away from his domestic base to an authoritarian institution and then regularly retraumatised by corporal punishment. The only possible result of this career of woe, Arvo argued, was the creation of a violent, emotional brute-psychotic with suicidal tendencies. If he had been that boy, he continued, and if he had been possessed of any objective sense, he would have put himself into the hands of another authoritarian institution, possibly a maximum security prison or *gulag*, or blown his brains out to save the tax-payers money.

Stagg reached the end of the letter and looked up. His mother was staring at him over the rim of her cup.

"Well, what do you expect me to say to this?" he said with a cutting laugh.

"Do you think there's any truth in it?"

"Why don't you use your own judgement?" Stagg asked her bitterly. "After all, you've known me for nearly fifty years. It might give you some idea."

"But that's exactly my problem, son: I don't know you. We've grown further apart since we've been together."

"Oh, don't talk such nonsense . . . " Stagg said wearily.

"The more I know about you the less I can tolerate it," Joyce continued, "and I made you, didn't I?"

Stagg threw his hands in the air and leapt to his feet, pacing around the room with Arvo's letter in his hand. He was so agitated and upset that he raised his knees to an unnatural height as he walked up and down and it looked to Joyce as if he were about to jump out of the window.

"Please try to talk coolly about it," she pleaded. "I'm so flummoxed."

"Why do you talk about me behind my back so much? And to a useless wreck like Arvo?" he demanded, slamming the letter down on the table under his hand. "Why do you undermine me?"

Joyce was tremblingly silent, her eyes on his large, splayed hand.

"Perhaps it's because in my heart I always wanted you to be . . ." She hesitated, unable to say what she intended.

"Well? Go on, go on!" Stagg yelled. "Say it!"

"Just like anyone else," she managed to say, the words falling lamely from her lips. "Just like Frank was."

Stagg laughed derisively, heaving the sound out with no warmth or humour. He leant over the table and tapped his chest.

"Listen, you stupid old woman, I'm as much like anyone else as anyone else is like me. And you've no idea what my father was like!"

"Don't talk to me in that way . . ." Joyce protested but he swept her interruption aside, his face mottled with anger, his long forefinger stabbing at her shoulder.

"Now, let's leave me to one side and talk about you," he said heatedly. "I'm beginning to think that you haven't got what it takes to educate yourself. You're devoid of the necessary intellectual and emotional resources. Whenever you get confused you don't ask whether it's your inability to work out an answer that's the problem, oh no, you revert to your dimwitted intuition. That's not the attitude of a mature person at all. That's the way a girl behaves, blaming everything on other people which, in your case, is always me!"

Joyce got to her feet, her head held back and her eyes flashing.

"I've never been so insulted in my life!" she declared haughtily.

"Good! And don't expect me to apologise."

"You haven't got the manners," Joyce said aloofly, turning her back on him and making her exit as Mrs Hankinson edged into the doorway, drawn by the raised voices.

Stagg watched the two women go then returned to his worksuite, lying in an uncomfortable bronze pea-pod armchair for three hours while he tried to think about something else, but his mother had the domination of his mind. That night, while the moon was high and beaming over the brakes and coppices and woods, while owls and foxes pursued their quarries, he rang his mother in her bedroom. There was no light in the eastern tower and he knew that he was waking her, but what he had to say was too important to wait until the morning.

"It's me," he said into the mouthpiece when she answered. "I'm ringing to apologise."

"It's twenty past three," came the measured response, "and you said that you weren't ever going to apologise."

"No, I didn't, actually. What I said was that you shouldn't expect me to apologise," he corrected her. "That's a different matter."

There was a pause as she worked out the rights and wrongs of his argument.

"All right. Let's say no more about it. Good night," she said finally.

"Do you forgive me?"

"Yes, I think so."

"You *think* so?"

"There's plenty of time to work all this out, son. We're both impetuous people. I'm not an easy woman to get along with, I know. As Moira says, we're both as bad as each other but the basic relationship can be salvaged if we keep our heads."

Stagg took a moment to register Mrs Hankinson's involvement in the modified form of absolution which he had received and was about to say something else but Joyce rang off and left him holding the receiver to his chest.

Chapter Eleven

The next morning Stagg's mother had not come down to breakfast by noon and she had not rung him in his work-suite. When Stagg asked Mrs Hankinson whether she had spoken with her, the daily help smiled wanly and pushed past him with the giant orange vacuum-cleaner.

"I knocked on her door but she told me to go away," she said. "She'll be working on her studies, I expect."

Stagg went up to the eastern tower. When he knocked and shouted his mother's name there was a scuffling but no reply. He opened the door slowly in order to give his mother time to prepare. When he got into the room he found her sitting on the edge of the bed, half-dressed, her breathing short, grey fatigue showing in her face.

"Oh, God," he groaned. "Why didn't you call me?"

With a gentle insistence he made her lie back on the bed. The Ventolin inhaler was gripped in her fist. He prised it away and rang the local doctor.

"It'll go away," Joyce croaked. "When I get no sleep it comes. My mind won't give me any rest."

The doctor came. When he had finished he came downstairs and found Stagg waiting in the hall. As he twirled his medical bag by the handle and gazed into an alcove harbouring a huge bluestone skull he told Stagg that, in his opinion, Hilbre was not a house to be ill in.

Stagg ignored the remark and quizzed the doctor about his mother's condition.

"At this stage," the doctor told him, "the bronchitis develops into a kind of asthma."

"What does that mean?" Stagg asked.

"Well, it can be brought on by many things — like allergies or upsets. Asthmatics have to be very careful. They're always walking on eggs, especially if they're in a weakened state."

When the doctor had gone, Stagg went upstairs and sat with his mother. She asked him to read to her.

"Anything in particular?" he asked.

"I've made a start on Freud's *The Interpretation of Dreams.*"

"Oh," Stagg said hollowly. "Why?"

"I've been dreaming a lot lately."

Stagg opened the book at the place where she had left a green plastic comb and began to read. It was turgid stuff for the human voice and he soon stopped, glancing round the bed for other books which he might turn to.

"I think I should take advice, Malcolm," Joyce murmured. "We'll talk about it tomorrow because I'm dropping off now. The quack gave me something." She put her hand out and took his. "I'm very disturbed, son. Can't forget what I did to you. I've been very disloyal. Someone's got to help me take the load off my shoulders."

"Are you saying that you want to see a psychiatrist?" Stagg enquired with trepidation. "I think you'd walk all over him."

Joyce smiled, already half-asleep.

"Perhaps the best thing would be for me to go back to living on my own," she sighed. "I did less damage that way."

"That's out of the question," Stagg told her sternly.

"You need your freedom, son, and, at my age, I need my peace of mind. There must be someone we can talk to together."

"Together?"

"Oh, yes, we'd have to be together . . . have to . . . "

She lapsed into slumber, her face relaxing into a peaceful mask. Stagg sat and looked at her, his eyes brimming. In all his life he had never watched her actually fall asleep. To hear that clear, strong voice tail off and see the troubles fly from her expression was a moving sight. If it was in his power to give her tranquillity like that, he would do so.

He spent the afternoon on the telephone. His own doctor in London did not know any self-respecting psychiatrist who would take on a mother and son as a group and those practitioners Stagg rang directly would not accept any dictation in the matter of how any consultations should be conducted. When he emerged from his work-suite at tea-time, he found Mrs Hankinson in the kitchen, her eyes reddened with weeping.

"You have to do something," she croaked dramatically. "That poor female is suffering."

Stagg could not help but agree: sitting at the kitchen table he ran his long fingers through his hair, shook his head, shifted his shoes around on the Cumbrian green slate floor, feeling himself drawn towards Mrs Hankinson. In an embarrassed, troubled voice he admitted that he, also, was very worried about his mother.

"And so you should be, Malcolm," she replied, "because she's very worried about you."

"That's what makes it difficult to handle," he pointed out lugubriously. "It's two people worrying about each other rather than getting on with their lives. She's already got me scouting round for a psychiatrist. I must say, I find the whole idea demeaning."

"Then you're being proud, Malcolm," Mrs Hankinson rebuked him. "There's nothing the matter with getting expert help from outside."

"But we're both perfectly sane!" he protested.

"Look at it this way," Mrs Hankinson said, clearing her tears with a long, determined sniff. "It's an unnatural situation we have here."

Stagg stared at Mrs Hankinson, an involuntary shudder travelling the entire length of his body, flooding his veins and nerves with ice. "What do you mean?" he said once the sensation had fled via his lifted scalp. "There's nothing unnatural about it at all."

Mrs Hankinson calmed him down and sat very close as she took him through the different stages of her thinking about Joyce.

"You've put her life into reverse by taking her to see her husband's grave, which made a kind of nonsense of the last fifty years for her, and by bringing her to live in this sarcophagus," she said.

"It's not a sarcophagus!"

"Malcolm, you're not being completely honest," Mrs Hankinson reproved him, frowning. "Everyone knows what this house represents. It's fascinating to anyone interested in art and architecture maybe, but not much fun for the mother of the complex man who created it, perhaps?"

Stagg could not keep his eyes off Mrs Hankinson's mouth. It was thin-lipped and had the firmness of the righteous. What I would give to kiss her at this moment, he thought to himself. She is going to tell me something new about myself at last.

"This house is your father," Mrs Hankinson informed him. "It's the strength which you missed. Can you imagine what it's like for a widow to live in her dead husband's memorial?"

"I never thought of it that way, I must admit," Stagg mumbled, lowering his eyes as the desire to kiss Mrs Hankinson faded, "and I reject the idea unconditionally, but has my mother ever said that she believes in that interpretation?"

Mrs Hankinson told him that, as far as she had observed, Joyce had not been able to assess her predicament fully. "But it is only a matter of time," she added, "and the more reading she does the more perceptive she will get."

Mrs Hankinson then proceeded to recommend to Stagg that he should not consider entrusting the case to a conventional psychiatrist but should allow her to use her influence with her old professor of Psychology at Bristol University who was chairman of a private mental health enterprise, a reputable company with a branch in Norwich which had a high success rate in dealing with all matters pertaining to emotional and spiritual health.

Stagg and his mother met Sam Cronin, the counsellor appointed to solve their problem, in his consulting-room at the company's premises a week later. Mind Minders was located on an industrial estate, sharing a half-developed plot with a thriving timber business. As Stagg sat down and looked over Sam Cronin's shoulder he saw a log hanging outside the window. When the burly counsellor caught the direction of Stagg's eyes he waved offhandedly.

"Forget them," he advised. "Concentrate on what's going on in here. There's a knot which has to be untied, then retied. That's how I see it. Would you agree with that, Joyce?"

She nodded, smiling affably as Sam Cronin thrust his fingers into his golden V-shaped beard.

"I've got two strong people here who are in a tangle," Sam Cronin continued, beaming. "That will give us a lot of energy-input and luckily we have plenty of leads already. We can make a start by saying, Malcolm, that I've already taken the trouble to drive out to see your house. Wow! What an ego-trip that is!"

"I'm an architect," Stagg retaliated immediately, his nerves on edge. "How else would you expect me to express myself?"

"Exactly!" Sam Cronin said triumphantly. "Keep hold of that! But also remember that it was your flagrant act of ego-building which launched your mother into a completely new and strange world. Whether you care to admit it or not, you designed and erected that paternal totem of male pride in order to punish your mother for sending you to that school. Now, what do you say to that?"

Stagg blinked and looked over Sam Cronin's shoulder. He could see a crane turning on its platform, the open jaws of its grabs flexing as they descended towards a load of teak on the back of a lorry. Stagg stiffened as his eye encountered a crest on the cab: a red tree with RUN KILL A SON ANGER HEALERS in scrollwork beneath it.

"Are you with us, Malcolm?" he heard Joyce say. "We're waiting for an answer."

Stagg remained in silence, staring at the cab of the lorry. He had decided not to speak until his mind started to behave itself.

"Hadn't you worked that out?" Joyce persisted. "It didn't take us long, did it, Sam? Only a few 'phone calls and we had it sorted."

"I think Malcolm is in shock," Sam Cronin said worriedly, getting up from behind his desk. "We may have gone too far too fast."

The words began to move as Stagg's brain slowly accepted its responsibilities to communicate the real world to his senses. He saw

138

the letters quiver until he could read: BRUNSKILL AND SON LUMBER DEALERS, then he turned to repudiate Sam Cronin's analysis of his motives for building his dream-home.

"I built my house in order to live in a place which satisfies me," he said quietly. "The world, in general, doesn't. It's ugly, malformed and unharmonious."

"Ah, so you dislike reality," Sam Cronin responded. "I see. Is there a reason you can give us for that?"

"There's too much of it," Stagg replied, his eye, once again, drawn to the crane which was now swinging a log across the heavens in a gravid arc which appealed to something deep inside him.

Joyce went to speak but Sam Cronin beckoned her to be silent, indicating that Stagg's reverie had to be respected.

"What are you thinking about, Malcolm?" he asked eventually.

"Matter in space."

"Shouldn't architecture have a human aspect?" Sam Cronin teased him. "I thought that was generally agreed."

Stagg took his eye away from the window and stared straight between Sam Cronin's ears, quartering his head in his mind. He noticed the shiny rebuilt nose and a scar just below the hair-line. It was a house of a face, lived in, repaired. When he measured each quarter against its neighbour's he discovered that the proportions were very unsatisfactory.

"Did you ever have a difficult birth?" he asked.

Sam Cronin wrinkled his brow, flashed a look at Joyce, then made a note.

"Are you feeling disturbed, Malcolm?" he asked, observing how Stagg was lacing and unlacing his long fingers.

"A house is born. It comes from a human mind so the character of it always has an association with people. I don't mind you ridiculing my character but I do object to setting up fake disputes about my artistic principles," Stagg replied. "It's very counter-productive to . . ."

Sam Cronin interrupted, cheerfully disavowing any such intention.

139

"But your art, Malcolm, is universal. It affects everyone. We have to look at it whether we like it or not. You can't hide in your shell and refuse to talk about it. Architecture is an affront to nature, or so it can be said. What we want to know is just what were you getting at when you built that house? Is it pure ancestralised male aggression?"

Stagg made no reply but his colouring deepened and he clumped his heels on the wooden boards of the floor a few times.

"Have you nothing to say? Are you only articulate when you have absolute power over the argument, as when you're building something? Can't we have a say? Talk to us." Sam Cronin rubbed at his nose and sighed, adjusting his squat thighs in his chair. "All right. Keep your secret. But I say, Malcolm, that to fling an insulting shape like your house on to the earth and then refuse to justify it is ducking the issue. Surely you must compromise to the degree that you'll explain it to us?"

There was another long, painful pause, then Joyce suggested that her son was silent because he could not give a reason for building Hilbre.

"Most people just buy a house," she said. "It's passed on from someone else. The best houses are the old houses. But he didn't want that because he doesn't want anything that's inherited, which includes me."

Stagg winced as he struggled to follow his mother's line of thought. In his mind he was attempting to resurrect the original stimulus for his design. He remembered Pythagoras, Vitruvius, Alberti and Fra Francesco Georgi, then Plato, Aristotle and the Bible, the mystic number 3 and its multiples, the visible symmetry of natural harmonic ratios, the human face, the human body, the horns of his dilemma, perfect consonance and the doubling of any string to make an octave, then his mind went blank.

"You do a lot of work behind what was once called the Iron Curtain, don't you?" Sam Cronin said soothingly. "Why is that, may I ask?"

"I go where the interesting work is," Stagg replied, "and why not? They seem to like my style at the moment."

"Your mother thinks that there's an association between that style of yours and the nature of the regimes which those people lived under," Sam Cronin explained slowly, his eyes on Joyce. "This perceptive woman believes that they like your work, which she doesn't, because they have a subconscious yearning to go back to the old oppressions of their childhoods. So, what's she's saying, is that you may be deforming the entire future of European architecture, and, basically, it's her fault."

Stagg turned his head to look at his mother. She was sitting very still and her profile was saintly, suggestive of suffering but severe.

"Where did you get that idea?" he asked as mildly as he could.

"I worked it out for myself," came the clipped reply. "Even if you can't think your way out of things, Malcolm. I can try."

"But you can't take on a responsibility like that!"

"I can if I think it's right and I've got the courage."

Sam Cronin raised his tufty eyebrows, encouraging Stagg and his mother to continue their exchange, which they declined to do. After a while he coughed then shuffled his papers before restarting his stalking of Stagg. "Joyce has explained to me about the traumatic effect that your display of egomania, by that I mean the building of Hilbre, had upon her entire existence. My argument . . . " he paused, cogitating for a moment with his forefingers pressed against the sides of his bent nose, "goes thus. This attack on you represents something benevolent, essentially. Your mother has, by the effect you have had on her, come to the point where she can constructively criticise you. This confirms her greatly augmented intellectual abilities and, I have to say, a breaking-down of any traditional barriers which might have existed as a result of her being your mother and you being her son. In my judgement you are now much more equal, which does reflect this trauma for trauma situation you two have got into."

Stagg made no reply. After a long, expectant silence Sam Cronin shrugged to express his disappointment.

"Let me put it to you this way, Malcolm," he said, "would you be prepared to dismantle your house for your mother's sake?"

"No, I wouldn't," Stagg replied nervously, glancing at his mother in case this refusal should bring on an asthma attack. "That's not on."

"Too much of a sacrifice?" Sam Cronin queried archly. "What are you prepared to do? First you destroy her self-confidence with that temple to your ego, then you make her your technical assistant. For a woman of her age to embark upon seven years training as an architect is a daunting proposition, but she's ready to do that if you approve. What do you say?"

Stagg sneaked another look at Joyce. She was holding her chin a little higher and he could see the whitened knuckles on her hands as she gripped her handbag.

"Is that what you want?" he asked. "Is that what this is all about?"

"It's the only thing which makes sense," Joyce replied drily, "as I think that your ideas are not serving contemporary society properly, and as I see you becoming increasingly influential, then it's my duty to stop you — which I can't as I could not hurt my own son — or provide the right competition which will win me the leadership in this field."

The cogency of her argument made Stagg lapse into silence. It was a new, threatening sign that her learning was starting to strengthen her mind as bronchitis weakened her body.

"This is all speculation," Sam Cronin said. "As I told Joyce, it strikes me that there's a very powerful and healthy bond between you. Don't forget, Oedipus didn't know that he was ruining his mother's life when he did. We can see things more clearly here."

"Yes, I see it clearly," Stagg affirmed, "but what I couldn't bear to think is that my mother has started to conspire against me."

Joyce clutched her handbag to her abdomen and let out her breath as if she had been struck.

"That's a very emotive word, Malcolm," Sam Cronin remarked sagely. "Let's not get into paranoia when I don't see it even on the horizon. Once your mother started thinking creatively this kind of situation was inevitable. And we've agreed, have we not, that you triggered the whole process by surrendering to peculiarly unfilial instincts to disturb the peace of her old age by building a monument to your own psychological disfigurements."

"All I wanted was for her to enjoy life," Stagg said morosely. "Not take mine over."

"Yes, yes," Sam Cronin enthused, "cling hold of the enjoyment motivation, but she must be free to eclipse you if she can."

"We talked about her going to university," Stagg continued lamely, "but I didn't imagine this."

His mother folded her arms and laughed curtly. "And what was I going to study?" she asked. "Can you remember?"

"Social sciences?" Stagg ventured though his mind had not provided a concrete memory. "Or was it English?"

"It wasn't discussed," Joyce said, implying a failure on his part. "He just kept saying, *university* with no real end in view.

Sam Cronin winked at Stagg and pulled out a fresh page of notes.

"You've got a very alert mother," he commented. "Not much gets past this lady. I suggested that she might study aesthetics then do some postgraduate research into the psychic subjectivism of the perception of beauty, but she told me to go to hell. Your mother wants to *build*, Malcolm. Are you going to be a help or a hindrance?"

Stagg thought that Sam Cronin had said asthmatics rather than aesthetics and it had frightened him into silence. The mind minder gave him a hard, critical look, clapped his hands together to signal the end of the session, then asked Joyce when her Estonian friend was due.

"Oh, about Christmas-time," she answered shyly.

"Then I'd better pencil in a couple of appointments. Christmas is a busy period for us all. From what you say, he'll need at least six visits. Are you going to come in on those sessions as well?"

Stagg stood up and went to the door. He would not remain to audit the remainder of their discussion, even though money was on his mind, particularly the question of who would be paying for this costly reformation of the post-Stalinist mental state.

A few weeks later Stagg was persuaded to go to Mrs Hankinson's house for Sunday lunch. There had been two more sessions with

Sam Cronin at Mind Minders and Stagg had to reluctantly concede that his mother appeared to be much happier and more stable with everything completely in the open between them. As his peace of mind decreased due to these exposures and investigations, hers proportionately increased. One feature of her improvement which irked him was that she insisted upon crediting Mrs Hankinson with saving her sanity and the woman was now canonised in the annals of the joint case "Stagg and his Mother", a clinical study of which Sam Cronin was writing up for *The Journal of Model Syndromes*. So, it was no surprise to Stagg when he arrived at the partially renovated Queen Anne mansion where Alec Hankinson carried on his furniture-making business, to find the stout mind counsellor already there, drink in hand. He was talking to a long-haired, dreamy-looking man, the lids of whose eyes were hardly open. As Stagg was introduced, he glimpsed a ghost, the nimbus of another personality behind the first impression.

"Malcolm," Alec said with a boyish smile, shaking hands so hard that his grey pigtail shook. "Glad you could come to lunch. Got a butcher's special. Aren't you totally staggered by the amazing coincidence?"

Stagg froze, leg muscles quivering, nostrils raised in the air. Before he could make a reply, Alec continued artfully: "My wife was washing down one of your filing cabinets recently and was frankly staggered to discover that we went to the same school. Didn't she mention it to you? How staggeringly secretive of her."

Stagg put his feet further apart to steady himself, the spectre behind his host emerging into the memory of a sly but cocky schoolboy.

"They called me Hank in those days. I did cross-country."

Stagg managed to say that he did not remember Hank, which was becoming more of a lie within the time it took to say it.

"Sam tells me that you have nothing but terrible memories of the old place," Alec burbled on blithely, "whereas I, who could run like a stag, but was no twelve-pointer, remember it with affection. In fact I'm an ardent old boy, very loyal, and I go down there for staggered visits every six months or so."

"I go too," Mrs Hankinson chipped in. "It's beautiful country-side."

"Maybe I misjudged it," Stagg murmured as he accepted a Venetian glass goblet of white wine from Alec, "I had forgotten the high standards of wit and repartee which made life worth living while I was there."

Unruffled and undeterred, Alec coasted smoothly into more persiflage, informing Stagg that there was an old boys' reunion in a month's time and suggesting that it might be good fun if they all went down together. "I think a lot could be achieved. We can all stay at the old Four Tuns which Malcolm will remember from the days when he used to canter round the back to get a pint of mild, and we'll have an excellent time. Perhaps you'd even consider playing for the old boys' rugby team? We always have a game against the current school first fifteen and don't disgrace ourselves. The Monarch of the Glen played lock-forward, didn't you?"

"What do you say, Malcolm?" Will you go?" Sam Cronin enthused. "It could help us a lot. Think of Joyce. And the nostalgia would do you good."

Stagg looked around for his mother but she had gone into the garden. He wanted to ascertain whether she had known about this proposal prior to their arrival that day. Her absence at that moment increased his suspicion that she had.

"What a marvellous stroke of luck, Alec being an old school friend! We must make every use of it," Sam Cronin exhorted him. "And it comes at exactly the right time. Haven't you noticed the difference in your mother lately? Isn't she much more secure, confident? We're making her into a remarkable woman. All it will take to set the seal on her cure will be a visit to the actual scene of the crime. With a little cooperation we could arrange to act out the punishments you suffered in front of her, providing that you've got the inclination to relive the trauma. Then, I believe, we'll have conquered her guilt and the future will look very rosy. She can qualify as an architect and go into partnership with you as a mother and son team. The fusion of styles should be fascinating. The other advantage is that if you die childless she can carry on with the business."

145

As Stagg held his head above this flood of suggestions and new provocations, a call came from the kitchen that everyone should go through to the dining-room. Stagg followed behind Sam Cronin who kept up his stream of prophecy and persuasion about Stagg & Stagg, Architects, and then he saw Joyce come through the French doors with a few stalks of lavender held to her nose.

"It's so good to have you here," Mrs Hankinson said as her husband served fish soup from a fluted old silver tureen with a heavy silver ladle. "I've always felt that we have so much in common. As you can see, we live a natural life with a lot of respect for the past and the earth, but it's not enough if you haven't got like-minded friends. The other people in Alec's craft are so dreary and phoney that we don't bother with them. I only went out to work as a cleaner because we needed fresh blood in our circle plus a bit more human entertainment. Another thing we'll have to do at the reunion is attend church. It's Anglo-Saxon, so sweet and intimate. Joyce tells me that you were a choirboy, Malcolm."

Stagg weighed the silver soup spoon in the palm of his hand before parting the parsley to get at the thick, orange liquid which was the fish soup. Yes, he confirmed, he had been a boy treble for two years, then an alto, then a bass.

"So you will have sung in that very church?" Mrs Hankinson mused, her lipsticked mouth making a trumpet-shaped channel for her soup. "Mmm, I bet you looked sexy in your cassock and surplice."

"I did," Stagg replied with a heavy grimace. "The village talent used to go mad in the pews. You know how girls lust after choirboys."

"Girls don't but matrons do, and clergymen, and male teachers," Mrs Hankinson whispered over her spoon. "Did he look angelic, Joyce?"

"I don't know. I never go into churches," Joyce replied. "What went on at that school is a mystery to me. It's strange that you never even showed me a photograph of you as a choirboy, son. You gave me pictures of you in the rugby team, the cricket team, the school play, all those, but not in your choirboy outfit. Why was that?"

146

"Sex is made dangerous by aesthetics," Sam Cronin intoned airily, using his heavy spoon as an illustration of the nubile curve. "Youth and art stir up madness. If humankind is ever to find its true purpose we must get away from the addictive pursuit of young-sters."

"What do you say to that, Joyce?" Mrs Hankinson asked. "You told me that you haven't had sex with anyone since 1942. Would a toy-boy get you going again or are you just glad it's all over?"

Joyce bowed her head over her plate and took the jolt which the question had given her. Moira was being less than sympathetic or sensitive but she knew that this was probably by design. The time had come to be relentlessly truthful about herself. Why should she not reveal all her most secret yearnings over lunch? What was so sacred about an old woman's memories?

"Robert Taylor was my pin-up," she announced, wiping her mouth with a heavy linen napkin which had The Clarence Hotel, Dublin stitched in one corner. "It would have to be someone like him."

"Who?" Mrs Hankinson asked.

"He was a film star," Alec explained, "tall, dark and handsome type."

"Ah, a fantasy," Mrs Hankinson said with a chuckle, fishing a mussel shell out of her soup. "Dead husband, dead film star, eh, Joyce? When are you going to come into the land of the living?"

"Modern men don't do anything for me," Joyce replied.

"You don't give them a chance to," Mrs Hankinson snorted, bringing a cock salmon's head to the surface of the soup so it appeared to be rising to a fly. "Joyce, darling, you're a vital living woman with fifty years of suppressed passion tearing around in your system. This Robert Taylor is dead."

"Well, I think he's dead," Alec muttered, stroking his chin. "Do you know if he's dead, Sam?"

"Robert Taylor? I haven't seen him in anything for a long time but that doesn't mean he's dead," Sam Cronin replied cheerfully. "But it means he's Hollywood-dead. In today's world which is the real death? Any takers?"

As there was no one who wished to pursue this question, Sam Cronin did so himself, providing the lunch-party with a long explanation of his theory of separate realities which was, he confessed, originally inspired by R.D. Laing's book, *The Divided Self*.

"My hypothesis is that the society we are moving into will become enthralled with self, and manipulative within Stagg-like images of self derived from egomania — of which Malcolm is a superb, classic example — and that a dissociation from physical reality will take place. Once this has happened we will be ready for the final phase in the artificialisation of the human species when its idea of itself will overtake the reality of itself and we will evolve into just a brain. The body will become obsolete."

Mrs Hankinson paused in the act of bringing the salmon head up again, leaving its milky eyes staring out of the soup.

"Do you mean a civilisation of pure thought?" she asked, hooking the ladle on to the edge of the tureen. "Only mental activities?"

"Rows of brains in battery sheds. Everyone lives off mental impulses. The rest of the work is done by robots. Food is thought and thought is food. That's what we're heading for: life as a cerebral adventure. Then the flesh will stop being master of the spirit, which is what I see as being the big problem today."

"What's made you think like this, Sam?" Joyce asked concernedly. "It's a very pessimistic opinion. Is it because you're so fat?"

"God, no," he scoffed. "That cures my ego. No, religion's failure has removed the anthropomorphic dream from the human imagination. We don't see the face of God any more, but we have taken back his brain. Why not? We donated it in the first place."

Sam looked pleased with himself. No one was interrupting him and he detected a muted respect amongst his listeners. It appeared to him that no counter-arguments would be forthcoming so he pressed on, his small, hairy hands making shapes in the air.

"It's the death of human society as we know it, Joyce," he said importantly, directing his speech at Stagg's mother who was hungry for every word. "Not that I don't think that the time is ripe for it. What a dirty, muddled fellow Man has been. Five thousand years of bloody turmoil and chaos. He's poisoned the planet. Murdered a fair percentage of his own species. Why? The flesh. Hunger. Greed. Blood-lust. I have no time for historical man at all. A waste of the earth's time. Give me the future and the cool brain. Let it be celibate if it likes!"

Joyce dabbed at her lips with her napkin, hurt by the swathe which the mind counsellor's scything thoughts cut through her ideas about life and meaning. She suddenly had a strong urge to kick him under the table.

"I don't think you really believe all that," she managed to say. "You're just making it up as you go along."

"No, no," Sam Cronin declared grandly. "I assure you, those are my feelings on these large issues. Man has failed to live within his corporeal dimension. He must abandon the flesh — and we can only hope that natural evolution will help us go in that direction — or wither as an animal species here on earth."

"I put this to you," Alec said, leaning over and ladling the salmon head into Stagg's bowl as his share of the second helpings, "if we came from the sea, as we're told we did, perhaps we'll all return there as brains in tanks of brine, and the cycle will be complete. Then what price sensuality, Malcolm, old boy? What price orgasm and joy? What price a smart spanking with a flexy old plimsoll?"

Stagg saw the trap that was being laid for him and began pushing the salmon head around his bowl as he worked on an oblique and tangential answer that would divert the course of the conversation. He was saved from further embarrassment by the entry of a small, brown emaciated man in a voluminous white overall who was the cook. He had cut the end of his finger off while chopping a carrot.

"Excuse me while I deal with this," Mrs Hankinson said, getting wearily to her feet and showing exasperation. "We have this kind of thing all the time. He will keep painting his fingers and unsighting himself."

Glad of a means to switch the subject of discussion away from Sam Cronin's structured pessimism, Joyce enquired for the reason why the cook kept painting his fingers.

"Oh, something religious," Mrs Hankinson replied. "I think it's to do with fertility."

She took the dazed little man back into the kitchen and left them to continue talking but Joyce had lost interest. She wanted to know about the cook. She had once been a cook herself.

"Nebuchadnezzar's an old friend," Alec explained, opening more bottles of wine. "He's a Zoroastrian Parsi from a minority tribe in Goa. I met him when he was working in a restaurant in Lowestoft. He was made redundant by this absolute bastard of a Punjabi who owned it, so we took him in. He's got no family, nothing. I expect he'll die here."

"He will at this rate," Joyce observed, her sympathies aroused. "How many fingers has he got left?"

"He's not much use, to be honest," Alec explained. "We don't let him do any actual cooking, only the preparation. Moira's very good with him."

"She's very good with everyone," Joyce agreed. "You know that they can sew bits on again these days?"

"Oh, I doubt if it's worth it at his age," Sam Cronin said gloomily, his spirits lowered by the sight of Nebuchadnezzar's blood which had dripped onto the parquet floor. "I went to Goa once. It was Portuguese, you know. Lots of crumbling baroque churches and poverty."

Mrs Hankinson returned and told them that Nebuchadnezzar was lying down with a tourniquet. Stagg watched his mother closely, knowing how quick her compassion was. She would want to know why the cook had not been taken to hospital. With horror he saw her accept the situation and the resumption of the talk around the table. When he raised the issue of Nebuchadnezzar's finger himself in order to provoke a response from his mother he was firmly admonished by Sam Cronin who had been getting into his stride on the subject of art, pain, God, death and the subjective basis of all human creativity.

"Malcolm," he said with rough vigour, "your attitude to architecture, to life *in toto*, is governed by the forces of your own traumatisation. You cannot face the agony of the human future because it is, in terms of your psyche, a repeat of the flagellation which you suffered in puberty."

"Quite right," Alec muttered, struggling to get a gas needle into a cork, "which is a damn good reason why you should face up to yourself, Staggers. Here you are, nigh on fifty, and still moaning about the perfectly justifiable thrashings you got at school. It's simply not on. Can't you accept that you needed knocking into shape? I remember you in those days, Staggers. The most unpleasant, belligerent boy in your year. Always fighting. Always beating people up. I can personally remember several clips on the ear which you gave me purely to amuse yourself." Alec grinned reproachfully and wagged the gas needle at Stagg. "Find some nobility. We all have to live with what we were. To have created a guilt-complex in your own mother because you couldn't come to terms with your past, well, I find that a bit thick, frankly."

Stagg could not find his voice. He looked over Mrs Hankinson's shoulder and through the French doors to the sunlit garden. His hand went slowly out, stiff and clumsy, until he could grasp the bottle nearest to him and he poured out a goblet of blood-red, jugular burgundy and raised it to his lips.

"Oh, Malcolm," Joyce sighed from the other end of the table. "You were always such a liar when you were a boy. I thought you'd grown out of it."

"Of course he hasn't," Mrs Hankinson chortled. "He's worse now. That's what happens in the professions. All they teach you is to be a better liar."

"That's too cynical a view," Sam Cronin said as the door opened and Nebuchadnezzar re-entered with his hand in the air. Mrs Hankinson had tied a piece of fuse wire around his wrist to stop the flow of blood and his hand had turned blue. While Mrs Hankinson loosened it there was a brief argument about business ethics, which neither Stagg nor Nebuchadnezzar participated in, both being dazed.

"The question is," Sam Cronin said as the little Goan tottered out again, "which came first? The beatings or the bullyings? Was it because he was being flogged so much that he took it out on the other boys by bullying them, or was it because he was bullying the other boys that he was flogged?" The mind counsellor paused, fixing Stagg with a bright, questioning eye, then added: "Now that everything is out in the open, perhaps Malcolm will tell us which interpretation is correct?"

There was a loaded silence around the table as Stagg moved about in his high-backed chair, turning his head to left and right like a pilot looking for the lever of his ejector seat. His spirit was sorely tried by the attack made on him, but he was dumb. He could not remember bullying anyone but neither could he remember why he had been beaten so much. There must have been a reason. But even though he could not bring it to mind, he had to defend himself.

"Was I ever punished for bullying *you*, Hankinson?" he demanded pugnaciously.

"Good Lord, no, not me. I never complained when I was beaten up. I wasn't a *split*," Alec replied with dignity.

"Do you recall any particular boy I bullied?"

"It's hard to remember anyone you didn't, except for boys bigger than yourself."

"Give me a name," Stagg insisted, lowering his head and rapping the table with his knuckles. "One name!"

"Well, I could give you the school register, virtually," Alec mused, a crooked smile on his lips, "but I'll give you one: how about Wazz Walsworthy?"

"Wazz Walsworthy?" Stagg exclaimed. "You can't be serious."

"You used to beat up Wazz Walsworthy a lot. He was always moaning about it; not to you, of course, because he was scared."

"But Wazz Walsworthy was one of my best friends!" Stagg protested.

"Exactly. The more that you liked a chap the more you beat him up. That's just your weird nature, Staggers. I believe that you are the same with your poor mother, but using mental violence."

Stagg could find no further words of repudiation. Anger was rising in his blood and he knew that for him to continue with the dispute might mean a loss of control. As he sat in silence, feeling his throat swell with rage under his collar, he had to listen to Alec accusing Wazz Walsworthy of being a *schmall*.

"Of course he wasn't!" Stagg snorted suddenly.

"And you were jealous of him," Alec persisted. 'If any fellow got too close to Wazz Walsworthy it wouldn't be long before there'd be a battle royal with locked horns and Staggers running amok all over the place."

With a stifled groan of contention, disgust and despair, Stagg turned his body from the table, holding up his head with one elbow on his place mat. This distortion of his past was twisting in his bowels, making him feel unreal. Wazz Walsworthy, so called because of his bird-like profile which had earned him *oiseau* from the French master, had, on leaving school, gone into the building industry and had been one of the betrayers who had let him down over the Estonian affair. To have to think about the man was bad enough, but to be forced to try and remember whether he had ever been sexually jealous of him, was too much.

"Certainly that's made him think a bit," Joyce commented after she had scrutinised her son for a moment. "But I have to say that he's never struck me as the jealous type."

"Ah, but a boarding-school is a torrid zone when it comes to any sexual bonds," Sam Cronin explained. "Every love is an orchid there."

Stagg threw his napkin off his lap and got to his feet. With all the dignity he could salvage from the flaming ruins of his self-esteem, he stalked around the table, opened the French doors and went into the garden. As he stood in the sun and heard the blackbirds sing, the conversation resumed around the table and he could hear his mother asking Alec for definitive translations of *split* and *schmall*. There was a tone in her voice which pained him deeply, the drone of a diligent but limited pupil gathering knowledge. It enraged him, but it was poignant. It was the sound of Joyce applying her mind, insisting upon her readiness to listen. There was nothing in the catacombs of the world's learning from which she would turn away, including this mummified lie.

"A *schmall*," he heard Alec saying, "was a boy who was a catamite."

"What's a catamite?" Joyce asked.

"Well, love, he gave his favours to older boys and masters."

"What kind of favours?"

"He was too weak to stand up for himself so he appeased the desires of people who had authority over him in order to make his life easier."

"Are you talking about sexual desires?"

"I am."

Stagg folded his arms as the pause hummed above the bees in the garden air. He did not disagree in any way with the definition of *schmall* so far. Alec's clarity of thought equalled his corruption of truth.

"And my son had a friend who was a *schmall*?"

"I'm afraid he did."

"Are you saying that the boy appeased my Malcolm's sexual desires?"

"No, I'm not," Alec replied carefully. Stagg gripped his hands together, desperate to lean round and look at his mother's reaction. "All I'm saying is that your son had a *schmall* for a best friend, which might have been the making of him."

"The making of who?" Joyce asked. And Stagg heard no reply.

Stagg was not a deceitful man. Whatever self-criticism had been created within his powers over life, he had never accused himself of that. Alec's baseless allegation of jealousy had been left unrefuted because Stagg had chosen not to debate it in front of his mother. From the open French doors of the Hankinson mansion he heard phrases drifting, sweetly suggestive of praise: "Dear old Staggers. He's a hard worker no matter what else you say about him" (from Moira Hankinson, and warmly said). "It will need a lot of guts . . . the imperative is honesty in this kind of situation" (author, Sam Cronin, with a golden, winey glibness). "He wrote to me every week. I still have every one of his letters from school, but no mention of all this business" (his mother, sticking up for him).

"But that's very male behaviour," Mrs Hankinson said, noticing that Stagg had edged himself back to the wall where he could hear better. "What I want to know is — why? I told my mother everything. As far as I was concerned she was, first and foremost, another woman."

"Well, a boy can't say that about his mother, can he?" Joyce piped up defensively. "He doesn't know anything about being a woman because he isn't one."

"Boys don't do that with their fathers either," Mrs Hankinson drove on her point, "in fact, boys don't tell anyone, anything. Now, I'd like to know why because I personally admire Malcolm very much. I think he's attractive, intelligent, cultured, civilised and sexy."

"Ach, you'd think Hitler was sexy," Alec growled. "I'm going to bring in this well-hung venison. Get Staggers back in here, will you?"

"He's gone, I'm afraid," Mrs Hankinson said, standing up to watch as Stagg went across the garden to a gate in the fence.

Stagg got in his car and drove away. Before he had gone a quarter of a mile he knew that he had to return to protect his interests and argue. Perhaps he had been wrong about himself? Had he forgotten his own past? He parked on the grass verge and walked back to the Hankinson mansion, leaving the road just before the drive and climbing through a hedge which gave him access to a copse which grew up to the garden wall. From there he got into the back garden, across a yard and in through a pantry window where he found Nebuchadnezzar standing at a deep stone sink with his wounded hand held in the air while, with the other, he washed a lettuce. Stagg paused as he noticed a mattress and an old sleeping bag with a broken zip on the floor and a dirty holdall stuffed with clothes beside them. He had intended to walk straight past without any explanation of his presence in the pantry but he found that he could not ignore the man in his own home.

"Is your hand any better?" he asked. "That must have given you quite a shock."

155

"What's a finger? It could have been my penis," Nebuchadnezzar replied, looking meaningfully at a faded colour photograph of Mrs Hankinson which was stuck over the sink.

Stagg shuddered and pushed past the mutilated Goan, climbing up a short flight of stone steps into the main kitchen. It was empty. He crept across the red tile floor and into a corridor which took him to a conservatory which was separated from the dining-room by a pair of folding doors. When he applied his ear to the hinged join he could hear the conversation which was still going on around the lunch-table.

"Furniture-maker? Him?" Mrs Hankinson's screech of laughter made Stagg stiffen at his post. "Upstairs is full of old sofas. He hasn't done a stroke of work for ten years."

"What d'you live off, then?" Joyce asked. Stagg could imagine the hard look in her eye as she asked this essential, primary question.

"Oh, family money, of course," Mrs Hankinson snarled. "His dad made hen-houses on wheels. Sold them everywhere. Argentina. Ohio. The Orange Free State. Didn't he, Alec? He was a proper man, his father. Energy, drive, virility. But his son here? What a different story. My husband is a failure, as I've often told him, haven't I, lover?"

"Many times, darling," Alec whimpered.

"And you should be punished, shouldn't you?"

"Yes, angel."

"You should be humiliated."

"Of course."

"That's how we redress the balance, Joyce, and keep him healthy."

Stagg frowned as he heard chairs being moved. He could imagine his mother witnessing this strange exchange and her confusion.

He heard Sam Cronin cough and mutter incoherently, then his mother started to say something but faltered. When she resumed her attempt to speak she was brusquely interrupted by the mind counsellor who seemed to have got his thoughts together after a struggle.

"You must understand that we want to help you Joyce. One has to be faced by the physical reality of what one fears, the unvarnished truth. I feel bound to tell you that it is my professional view that, in your case, everything must be pushed to the limit. We have not much time so we can't pussyfoot around. When I was fourteen my father, who was a Plymouth Brother, table-ended my mother in front of my eyes. When the magistrate asked him why he'd done this he said that he'd only wanted me to know the truth about how I'd been begotten; in sin, lust, filth and shame. So, one thing I do know a little bit about is the effect of trauma on the adolescent mind and the danger of the obsessive ego."

Stagg heard a man sob. He was not sure whether it was the teller or Alec Hankinson who had made the sound. In the pause which followed Sam Cronin's brief autobiographical moment and the sob he heard the sound of his mother nervously clearing her throat. Then Sam Cronin spoke again: "It's really why I first went into mental reconstruction work. It made me completely unafraid of dark places. My mind can take anything."

Stagg listened intently. He was sure that his mother would respond, condemning this obscene trickery. It struck him that her reactions were getting slow as she had not immediately rejected the chicanery behind Sam Cronin's table-ending saga—a tale which had shaken Stagg considerably.

Then he heard Mrs Hankinson rap out a sharp command that all hands should come on deck to witness punishment, followed by an answering whimper from Alec. Mr Hankinson then shouted: "Stand by for chastisement!"

Stagg's heart started to pound as he recognised the vibrant, thickening timbre of the woman's voice. He took a few steps back then shoulder-charged the folding doors and burst into the dining-room as the bells of panic clanged in his head.

He found Alec Hankinson bent over the dining-table with a large bone-handled carving knife in his hand, starting to cut into a haunch of venison, steadied for him by Sam Cronin. Behind Alec stood his wife, her round eyes glittering with frenzied delight, a cat o' nine tails made of black rubber strips of upholsterer's webbing held above her head.

Without a word Stagg picked his mother up out of her chair and carried her bodily out of the house.

Chapter Twelve

It was his mother's claim to have been brought back to full mental and physical health by her Sunday lunch experience at the Hankinsons that pushed Stagg over the edge. He became very depressed, convinced that Joyce was being alienated from him with every step that she took along the path of enlightenment. She was now in the camp of the enemy, refusing to see the Hankinsons and Sam Cronin as corrupt sophists and perverters of knowledge, insisting that these mountebanks were genuine pioneers of human truth. Stagg could not abide this brand of indiscriminate intellect-ualism. He told his mother that it was tantamount to playing a game with her sanity. She replied that experiment was no crime of the heart but his over-reaction to the domestic gambolling of the Hankinsons in their own dining-room was. It revealed a trait in his character which she did not like. The labels which Joyce attached to this fault in him were starchiness, hypocrisy, sanctimoniousness and prunishness. Upon hearing the ultimate epithet Stagg immedi-ately assumed that his optical malady was now affecting his hearing. It did not occur to him that Joyce could be throwing out a few inspired new verbal creations as she continued her struggle with the English language.

Stagg decided that the only cure for his enervating melancholy was to leave Hilbre and take a long rest. He told his mother that he had to go to Finland on business, but privately arranged with an admiring client of several years past to take up an invitation to spend a holiday in his dacha situated in the midst of the Finnish lakes. Joyce wanted to accompany him but Stagg refused, making the excuse that the project which he would have to work on involved the construction of a military subterranean command post beneath the Arctic Shield and anyone over the age of sixty-five was barred from the area. The complete absence of any logic in this prohibition seemed to convince Joyce and she let him go with her blessing but many doubts about whether he should prostitute his talent by working for the obsolescent armed forces of any nation now that the world was progressing towards pacifism.

Stagg took his leave, compounding the untruths which he had already told by saying that he would only be away for a couple of weeks. It was his intention to be in Finland for at least a month, longer if he could manage it. He did not care very much what happened to his house or his business during that time. Money was left for living expenses, the bills were paid, the answering-machine was turned on in the work-suite, and he went, taking the car ferry from Harwich to Hamburg and from there to Trave-münde on the north German coast to catch a ship across the Baltic to Helsinki.

On the day of Stagg's departure Mrs Hankinson was there to see him off, standing next to Joyce outside the front door as he grimly drove off.

"Malcolm has a lot on his mind," Joyce said as Mrs Hankinson opened the front door for them to go back inside. "I hope he sorts himself out while he's away. He's been very low lately."

"Did he leave you a reading list?" Mrs Hankinson asked as they went into the kitchen.

"Oh, yes. I made him do that."

"What's on it this time?"

Joyce opened her handbag and took out a sheet of paper with a list which Stagg had typed out that morning before his departure.

"William Cobbett's *Advice To Young Men*," she read out.

"Well, that's not a lot of use to you, is it?" Mrs Hankinson protested.

"Malcolm thinks that I've got to make more effort to understand his kind of maleness. He told me last night that I was falling into the clutches of harpydom."

"Harpydom?" Mrs Hankinson echoed, filling up the electric kettle. "Whatever can he mean?"

"That's what I said. He just told me to look it up."

"Did you?"

"No, I got too involved with William Cobbett and I don't want any tea, thanks, or coffee. It makes you into a slopkettle, William Cobbett says."

"I've never heard that word before," Mrs Hankinson replied, sitting down. "Sounds wonderfully insulting."

"There was a time when ordinary people didn't drink tea and coffee all day. I expect I'll backslide but I'd like to imagine what it was like to be not always pouring that stuff down your throat. Why do we do it, Moira? Right now I find the thought very irritating that my nerves need stimulation of that sort. For the sake of my mind I must try to give all that up and make a fresh start." Joyce's voice tailed off as she watched Mrs Hankinson put a tea-bag in a cup and poke it down into the boiling water with a fork.

"What else is on your list?" Mrs Hankinson asked as she lifted the battered tea-bag out and flipped it into the sink.

"He wants me to read all the Bible, *The Decline and Fall of the Roman Empire*, Tolstoy's *War and Peace* and Burton's *Anatomy of Melancholy* in three volumes, if I've got time."

"How long did he say he was going away for?"

Joyce looked at the surface of the kitchen table. The grain of the wood was whorled and knotted with flowing, natural tramways which had often entranced her mind in idle moments. She stared at them now, hypnotising herself so she would not answer Mrs Hankinson's question with any honesty.

"He said a fortnight," she whispered.

"But you think it will be longer?" Mrs Hankinson suggested, her pencilled eyebrows raised.

"Yes."

"And I think you'll be right. Your little boy has run away from home, I suspect."

"I know, and it's his own home. That's what makes it worse."

Joyce ran her finger along the grain of the wood, following one line through all its meanderings, skirting the dark discs of the knots. It was the blood-line of sonship to her.

"I've driven my lad out of his creation," she sighed.

"Nonsense!" Mrs Hankinson scoffed, picking up the daily newspaper and opening it with a flourish. "Malcolm does as he likes."

"It has to be said that it might be justice. After his first divorce he sold our old home, which he'd bought cheap and with my agreement and my mother's, and I had to go and live in a council flat."

Mrs Hankinson lowered the newspaper and regarded Joyce with an incredulous eye.

"You what?" she exhaled noisily, putting the newspaper down on top of the table. "He did what?"

Joyce shifted uncomfortably in her chair and looked sheepish.

"I shouldn't have told you that," she murmured, "it just came out without thinking."

"The bastard!" Mrs Hankinson squealed. "The sod! Why did you let him, for God's sake? Did he send in the bailiffs to get you out?"

"No, no, it wasn't like that," Joyce corrected her hastily. "I agreed to him selling it. He needed the money and the house was much too big for me. Also my mother had just died in it and I was becoming quite morbid, if you know what I mean. I liked being with her presence. Malcolm said that was unhealthy."

"I bet he did!"

Joyce got up and made herself a cup of tea, standing by the kettle and watching her distorted reflection in its curved side.

"Well, it's no wonder he's got on in the world," Mrs Hankinson said, going back to her newspaper.

"Yes, but if you think about it, Moira, if he bought the house there was obviously going to be a time when he'd sell it," Joyce murmured apologetically, regretting that she had brought the whole thing up.

"He could have waited until you'd died."

Joyce's hand holding the cup and saucer shook until they rattled. She sat down on the edge of the table.

"That's the thing, Moira. He couldn't do that. To him it was like putting me in a tomb. He didn't want to imagine my death in any way. So he sold it . . . " She stopped talking and put the cup and saucer down beside her with elaborate care. "And now I live in this place which is his life."

Mrs Hankinson stood up and joined Joyce, putting her arm around her.

"Have you just realised this?" she asked.

Joyce nodded.

"If I'd stayed in that house I wouldn't need to have died. I'd have been dead already, living off memories. He knew that was wrong."

"Will you tell him all this when he gets back?"

"He knows it already. What he doesn't know is how I've talked in such a way to people that I haven't been able to make it clear," Joyce replied, the worm of self-disgust busy in her bowels. "I'm so ignorant, you see, Moira. I couldn't explain to people about how my son felt about death. Why not? What's the matter with me? How can anyone love you more than wanting a full, exciting life for you? The boy had seen my misery, my obstinacy . . . oh, Moira, what a woman I've been."

Mrs Hankinson had expected Joyce's tears and was glad to help. She gave consolation as they sat side by side on the kitchen table, recalling her own abnormal affection for the trappings of death at the time of her father's decease and the long months it had taken her to shake off this silky, insinuating morbidity which defeated joy at every turn.

"Joyce, I had a taste for death," she prattled solicitously. "I was a complete addict, listening to all those pontificating old crows who advised me to wallow in my grief, God, why didn't they say *enjoy* it? Grief is a thing to be got rid of, I say. We've got too short a time on earth to spend it all that way. Joyce, you have to face it. Your grief over your mother's death would have strengthened your long-standing grief at the loss of your husband and together they'd have destroyed you. Malcolm was right."

"And he did need the money," Joyce sniffed, "that does have to be born in mind."

"Yes," Mrs Hankinson said with some irresolution, feeling that she had got carried too far by her enthusiasm. "It was probably six of one and half a dozen of the other."

In the long days that followed, Joyce increasingly missed her son and began to feel an irrepressible desire to contact him. He had not left any address or telephone number and all her efforts to track down the site of a subterranean army command post under the Arctic Shield through the War Office, NATO and the Finnish government met with no response other than colossal telephone charges on Stagg's account. In her frustration she wrote him several letters which revealed her deepest feelings about their relationship and took them in her handbag to the old boys' reunion. She stayed at the Four Tuns with Alec and Moira Hankinson and attended most of the functions over the long weekend, including the rugby match and the dinner-dance where she did a quickstep with the headmaster. He was an affable man, very urbane and smooth, but his composure was shaken when he discovered that he was dancing with the mother of Malcolm Stagg, the famous architect. As far as prominent men produced by the school were concerned, Stagg was the most distinguished; in fact, such was the paucity of the list which the headmaster had been able to pore over while composing the recent school prospectus that he knew Stagg was the only one with any reputation at all.

"I must say, Mrs Stagg," he said as they circled the floor, "it is very unusual for a parent to come to this weekend. Perhaps we should start an association for you as well?"

"Do you still have my son's records?" Joyce asked, enjoying the sensation of all her old dancing skills returning to her body. "There's something I'd like to check."

"I think we have those for every pupil who was ever at the school," the headmaster replied.

"Would you let me have a look at Malcolm's, please?"

The headmaster smiled uncertainly, holding himself away from his partner and communicating his moment of alarm to her.

"May I ask why? Surely Malcolm has no need of any references which we might be able to give from such a long time ago," he said.

"I want to see just how many times he was beaten," Joyce declared, assuming the lead of the dance as the headmaster's authority faded in her arms. "The records would show that, wouldn't they?"

"Not necessarily," the headmaster replied, retrieving his proper role as the guiding force in the quickstep. "From my perusal of the archives I'd say that records were not kept of every punishment meted out."

"Oh," Joyce said, lowering her chin, "I'm disappointed."

They danced on in silence, then the headmaster asked if she thought Malcolm might agree to come to the school to talk to the pupils about his work. Joyce hummed and hawed before answering that her son was quite a shy man but he might be persuaded.

"If he did come then he'd want his psychiatrist to be with him, and I'd have to be in the party as well because we go to sessions together," she added. "He was traumatised here as well as educated."

The headmaster dropped the idea of Stagg's visit and excused himself before the end of the quickstep. Joyce saw him talking to the fat man who had given the main speech at the old boys' reunion dinner. Both men kept glancing in her direction, then the fat man left the headmaster's side and came over to Joyce and requested a dance. She consented and they took the floor.

"You are Malcolm Stagg's mother, I believe," he said carefully as they moved into the modern waltz. "How good of you to come."

Joyce adjusted her hold on his arm in order to put greater distance between them as the fat man had no rhythm, only an urgent, forward posture which pushed her round the floor like snow in front of a snowplough.

"Did you know my son when he was here?" she asked, moving backwards with dainty steps.

"I did indeed. We were quite good friends," he breezed gustily. "Yes, old Malcolm has gone a long way since the old days. Good luck to him."

Joyce examined his face. Behind the thickened flesh of his jowls and cheeks she could see the shape of a wild creature. The nose of the man clinched it for her. It was a beak.

"Were you ever a *schmall*?" she demanded.

The man, who was a leading light in the old boys' association and a town councillor in his home district, did a full turn which made Joyce protest that he was doing an old-fashioned and not a modern waltz. When she attempted to restate her question concerning whether he had ever been a *schmall* or not, he made his apologies and hurried away.

Joyce found the headmaster hiding in the library and continued her interrogation. After a few minutes he decided to humour her rather than discourage this aberrant behaviour in a parent from the distant past, and they spent a while discussing the uses and abuses of corporal punishment, a means of discipline which was no longer employed at the school.

"Our psychiatrist believes that it was the beatings which gave Malcolm his talent," Joyce assured him, "but if that's the case I'd rather have had an ordinary child."

"I think most parents would agree with you, Mrs Stagg," the headmaster said patiently, his eye on the glass doors through which he could see Wazz Walsworthy entering with Alec Hankinson to rescue him. "But I do find that analysis rather lurid."

"If we'd stayed in Liverpool together and Frank had come back from the war, well, I reckon it would have been life at Aldershot or some army camp for all three of us. Frank loved the services, he was never happier," Joyce mused, her eyes running along the book-shelves where thousands of old copies of *Punch* were stored in battered covers. "And d'you know, I don't think Malcolm would have become anything out of the ordinary if that had been the story of our lives. He would have married a nice girl and had children and lived not far away. Of course, he would never have come here."

Alec arrived and informed Joyce that he was leaving to go back to the pub with Moira and a few old friends for a nightcap. Joyce shook the headmaster's hand and departed. On the way down to the Four Tuns she asked Alec if he would show her the actual places where Malcolm had been beaten.

"Oh, come off it, Joyce!" Alec protested. "You don't want to go that far, do you?"

"I do," she replied firmly. "It's an exorcism."

The next morning he took her to the housemaster's study at the Junior House and permission was obtained for the party to enter for a nostalgic visit, the present incumbent of the post being elsewhere at the time. Joyce looked around and drew the air of the place into her nostrils.

"He got a lot of it here?" she asked.

Alec grinned and affirmed that this was so.

Joyce opened her handbag and took out tightly folded packets of papers tied up with thin, red ribbons; the type of bundle which can be found thrust into the stonework of Greek and Spanish rural shrines to this day.

"What is it, Joyce?" Mrs Hankinson asked deferentially. "Can I help?"

"Malcolm's left home and I don't think he'll ever want to come back. I've written him some letters which I can't send him because I can't get an address," she said solemnly. "They're burning a hole in my pocket and I must get rid of them somehow."

"Oh, my poor dear," Mrs Hankinson oozed blatantly. "What a to-do. I've never known such a pair."

"It's the Irish in me," Joyce sighed as she got down on her hands and knees and looked under the desk, "and Robert Graves says it works."

In later years painters, decorators and builders who worked on renovations and alterations of the school's premises would find Joyce's votive bundles stuffed under floorboards, up chimneys and behind radiators in the rooms which she visited that day. When those plain working men untied these papers and studied them in future times they would be conscious of looking into a sacred, private world between mother and son which, though eye-opening, would be familiar. Nothing which Joyce had written down would, as men, astonish them. They would enjoy her candour and her innocence, also her energy, the writing of long letters having been long superseded in their experience by the use of the telephone. What might upset them would be the character of the son who loomed between the lines, an uncontrollable over-powerful phantom, born to plague the woman who had born him, an inveterate shit-stirrer and trouble-maker, a son doomed, like themselves, in their own relationships with their female parents. But then, in moments of honest self-examination, they would have to admit that it is not for nothing that the male is flung from the mother's womb in pain and never gets over it, whereas the girls simply submerge the event in their own menstrual rhythms.

One of the most popular-to-be of these letters read thus:

My dear Son,

My problems have changed as the years have gone by. You remain one of them but many things have altered. Once I thought that it was my duty to watch you grow up and become independent. This was made easy by your education which took you away from me, but then I realised that even education cannot alter the fact that when you've grown up it's what you were born with that matters.

We are still very close after all these years. You haven't drifted far, but now I think you must treat me differently, more as an equal. All I need is the belief that we are made of the same stuff, mother and son.

I know that you always wanted me to get married again and worked very hard at getting me fixed up with every man who seemed eligible. We won't go into some of the embarrassments which I had to endure at your hands, or the number of ugly chaps you had me all lined up to wed. I've always been a bit fussy about who I sleep with. But I do feel sorry that you had to do without a father and I was the only one who could have fixed you up with that. Sometimes I wonder whether even at this late stage you're still hoping that a nice chap will come along and take me off your hands. I'm afraid, son, I know that my next appearance at the altar will be in a box.

When I was widowed I started to have dreams for the first time in my life. I don't care what people say, before that I had never seen anything in my sleep but darkness. Here's one: I was with Frank at a dance, all dressed up. There was an orchestra. I was wearing a corsage of flowers. Frank's hair was in waves and he wore patent leather shoes and a white suit with wide revers. The tune never changed and we did the same dance all the time. It was a slow foxtrot. Everyone in the orchestra was black like Louis Armstrong but they had no proper faces. The music was visible as it came out of the saxophones as showers of red rain. As I danced with Frank he got smaller and smaller until I was holding him like a baby. When I looked closer I realised that it would be you, my unborn child.

What I'm trying to say, and probably confusing you, is that your imagination must have come from somewhere and I think it was me. Cissy has always said that it must have been from Frank, who left school when he was fourteen to work on the docks and never found out whether he was bright or not, but I think she's wrong. Frank was not a man of imagination, he was a child. His innocence was the most beautiful thing. With all the troubles of his life, having no father, his mother having left him behind to go to America, being poor, he thought life was a great idea. When he died there were many letters from people who knew him. In those days we called him Sunny because that was his nature, which was why my dad hated him to the core. How could anyone with any brains be so cheerful? He often said that Frank was an imbecile, but he wasn't. And the war could not change him, which made my father hate him even more. Now I've read things and remembered what my mother told me about the First World War, I think it was very different for the men. My father's life in the trenches was nothing like Frank's in the desert. But men aren't very intelligent about comparing their experiences. Competition breeds lies and my father fell foul of it. If Frank could come out of it all and shine like the sun, why couldn't my dad have the same power? When Frank was dead and I started using my imagination to build him up into even more of a saint, well, what chance did we all have? The truth had become as impossible as Frank. I couldn't tell it to you, I couldn't tell it to my dad, and I couldn't tell it to myself.

To the women of my sort of background it didn't matter which war it was took the men away. War was a god and it was a mother's job to feed it. When a son was born the mother's thoughts soon came round to wondering if he'd be taken. It was the nightmare of every mother until they stopped the call-up. In the minds of women of my age that fear still lives. I know that everything has changed now. Girls don't have that to think about any more and it must have changed our sex. When I see you going round the world putting up designs which you've created, I wonder if those buildings stand there because of me and those lies the war made me tell. Only you know the answer to that and I expect you'll keep it to yourself.

Well, I've made my excuses. Soon I hope to be free of the past and at peace. I know that you want me to enjoy the rest of my life and I'm certainly going to give it all I've got.

Which brings me to a terrible confession which I've discussed with Moira and Sam and they agree that it's time that I came out with it. When you were eighteen and I was still less than forty I used to go out with you and fantasise that you were your father. I was still a good-looking girl and I could sometimes get away with people thinking you were more than my escort and you knew what I was doing. Not once did you tick me off, though I knew that you were squirming. To have used you in that way for the convenience of my vanity was cruel and I have to ask a special absolution for that. What hurt you was the waste of my best years, I know, but I was rubbing salt into the wound with that kind of play acting.

Well, I hope you're having a good time behind the Arctic Shield. The michaelmas daisies are starting to come out and your greengage tree looks as though it might bear quite a lot of fruit. There's a stack of mail for you, most of it window-envelopes and advertisements. I think there're some from Peru, USA, Egypt and Japan. I've put it all in the office. Give us a ring from your secret base when you have time.

Your loving mother.
Joyce.

P.S. Before I go I thought I'd let you know that I've decided not to become an architect. After long talks with Moira, Alec and Sam — who've all been most helpful — I've gone for anthropology instead.

Chapter Thirteen

Stagg only lasted ten days in the silver birch woods where his
Finnish friend had his dacha. They fished, they walked, they took
saunas and drank beer. Evenings were spent talking around a
barbecue fire, the insects hovering just outside the protective aura
of a perfumed repellant which made Stagg feel like the Whore of
Babylon. The Fin, Fredrik, was accompanied by his wife and two
teenage daughters and it was the presence of the women which
drove Stagg out of the wilderness for day trips in his car, alone,
while the family swanned away their late summer. To be near
them was too stirring, too provocative to his blood. If he had
given his instincts their full sway he would not have wasted any
time talking to Fredrik. These quiet, respectful females, light as
saplings, would have bent to his breeze, not in passion but in
audience. Stagg had entered into the mysterious state whereby all
women are priests of the male spirit and speech with them is a
divine drug. Fredrik was a soft, reserved father and an ideal
husband, gently protective, and he would never have understood
Stagg's needs for the confessional. So there was no alternative but
the road. When he returned each night he saw to it that he kept
away from the women and sat apart with Fredrik, drinking and
talking under the pale northern night.

On one such trip he drove to Helsinki to stay for a couple of
days and view the much-admired twentieth-century churches
built by Finnish architects. Before he had left England an offer had
been made to him by the Church of American Bethany to design a
chapel in a Californian ski resort, a playground of the West Coast

rich. Stagg had not decided whether to accept or not, ecclesiastical projects having been outside his purview until now.

He saw the giant, pink single-breasted Kallio Church, which he found over-developed in its upward thrust; and the Temppeliau-kion Church in its handbuilt bomb-crater, lying like a flying-saucer which had failed to pull up before landing. Both had their beauties and he enjoyed the sweet Finnish spirit which strung itself throughout the stone, but they were not what he was after. He rang Fredrik and told him that he was going to drive northwards to Tampere to see the Kalevan Kirkko, a building which had excited one of his colleagues when he had visited the town. This proved to be a haunting shell, a softened cylinder which tempted Stagg into the dream of the hotel of God, somewhere for travellers on the earth. The design of Reima and Raili Pietila's church was a blend of husband and wife, he was told by his guide, of man and woman, all in flux and resolution, a harmony. To Stagg it was more of an irony that such a building should have lines which synthesised Hiltons and Sheratons all over the globe. His church, he decided, would go as far as a neon sign which flashed over the mountain-tops, offering God's hospitality, at a price. With this concept filed away in his working mind he began his return to the dacha but when he reached the turning off the metalled road on to the dirt-track which led into the silver birch woods, his need for Fredrik's women assailed him and he knew that his return would turn out badly. Without looking at the map he drove on, avoiding roads which would take him west, ending up that night in the town of Porvoo on the coast of the eastern Gulf of Finland. He found a small hotel and had dinner, then walked the deserted streets under brilliant stars. When he returned to his room he began drawing sketches of his church, filling the waste-paper basket with rejects as his irreverent irony eased and the images of the churches he had seen sank into his mind, displacing his desire to affront and leaving in its place a yearning for fusion.

When he went out for a walk in the town the next morning after breakfast he saw the homely dimensions of the place. It was a little port which had lost its trade and was now a dormitory for Helsinki commuters. In the morning it was emptied of men as they left the town for work, leaving women and children behind. As he went from street to street he began to look out for other males. Was he the only one? Pressure built up in his spirit, forcing him to return to the hotel, to an interior world as the exterior was devoid of his gender. Upon his arrival he found only women again, all calm, all in control. As he entered his room he found a female cleaner looking at the abandoned sketches which she had emptied from his waste-bin into her black plastic refuse sack. He held the door open and indicated that he wished her to leave at once.

Later on that morning he rang Fredrik to tell him the lie that he had been so taken with the Kalevan Kirkko in Tampere that he had stayed over in order to see how it looked in the early morning light. This was a fine, aesthetic reason which Stagg knew his friend would appreciate but, as he spoke, his heart tightened. Fredrik would tell his women and they would know yet one more secret about him: that his life was governed by the delights of the senses. When he returned to the silver birch woods and the shining water they would cluster around him and ask to be looked at in the early morning light, tall as steeples, as holy as any pilgrim's hotel. He would have to admit them into his heart and that was pointless. How could he love them? How could he afford them the worship which his pressing, pagan mood demanded?

At the hotel desk he saw a brochure of local tourist attractions. There was a late medieval church and the home of a great Finnish writer whose work was not known to him. The church was set on a hill, looking over deep river valleys which flowed a short distance to the sea. Set in the walls were fragments of older buildings, conglomerations of maleness which had been deliberately preserved to demonstrate antiquity. Stagg averted his eyes from these marks of accreted age. When he got inside and found hoary gospel-makers painted on the walls of the nave he raised his voice against them, and their scrolls. Nowhere in this universe, he said, is another me. All men are alone, so keep your visions.

Down in the lower town he went to the house of the writer,

Johan Ludwig Runeberg, which was a substantial single-storey residence of some charm in a quiet street. The woman who sold him his entrance ticket to the museum of the writer was compactly built, shapely, with chestnut hair and refined Tartar features, having broad, high cheekbones and sloe-black eyes set in an oval face of divinely alien allure. When, with his hand on the exit door, Stagg asked her out to dinner, she said no, causing him spiritual desolation. Ten minutes later he reappeared and bought another entrance ticket, four postcards and an emblazoned ashtray. The Tartar followed him round his second circuit of the property, thinking that he could be an English eccentric who might break something. As they stood side by side looking at the bed where the unfortunate Runeberg had spent nine years on his back, cared for by his devoted wife, Stagg began to make noises in his throat.

"What is the matter?" The Tartar asked, putting herself between the bed and Stagg. "Are you going to vomit?"

"All that suffering," Stagg said with a sigh. "It gets to you. Him lying there, his wife flitting about. What a life."

"They were very brave."

"Yes, they were, but it must have been hell."

The woman looked at him afresh. That morning had been a test of her stamina. For two months she had done this work, showing visitors around this tomb, selling tickets and brochures, opening up and shutting down. It was only a vacation job but the boredom had become unbearable precisely at the point where Stagg had appeared on the doorstep with a light in his eye. His approach had been at fault, far too urgent and humourless, but once she had turned him down doubts had set in. What else was she going to do in Porvoo that night? Two hours of voice practice. A bath. Watch television. A walk to the Saint Elmo's Fire Wine Bar? The tedium of a long summer vacation in Porvoo hit her.

"I'll have dinner with you on one condition: You don't talk about Johan Ludwig Runeberg," she said. "I've had enough of him."

Stagg's face lit up. He had not expected anyone in this emasculated town to feel for him. He had made a pass at her because she reminded him of an exotic madonna peeled off the wall of an orthodox church, lovely, and merciful. No real woman had ever looked like this except in the tents of the Khans where she would be concubine and goddess, charged with forgiving all males their plundering ways. As he looked at her she casually scratched between her breasts which brought him back into his own time and his own hopes for redemption.

When Stagg rang from Lapland to talk to his mother, she was showing Mrs Hankinson out of the front door. Stagg first asked if the messages from the office answering-machine could be listened to and noted because he had mislaid his remote interrogator; then moved on to his mail. Joyce waited until all the business was over before enquiring how he was and where he was.

"That's a long story," he said.

"Then tell it to me."

Mrs Hankinson signalled to Joyce that she would go and listen to the office answering-machine and bring Malcolm his messages before he rang off. This would only be a brief task for her as she had listened to them every day since Stagg had left.

"Moira says hello, by the way," Joyce said, waving to her friend as she hurried excitedly down the corridor. "She's gone to get all your messages."

"I thought I told you not to let her into my office?" Stagg said. "You know that I don't like her nosing around in there."

"Moira's been a good friend," Joyce replied, sitting down with the telephone cord fully extended. "I've been run off my feet with Ali and Yasouf staying here and all the coming and going."

There was a silence at the other end of the line. Joyce crossed her legs and looked out of the window.

"It's a beautiful day here. What's it like wherever you are?" she said.

Stagg looked at the telephone. It was the most unsatisfactory instrument when it came to the vital communications of a complex life. What were two Tunisian immigration officers doing at his house? If he asked for the information would his mother be able to convey the full circumstances? He decided not to ask.

"The temperature here is pretty low," he stated.

"They've started a business exporting Bedouin rugs into the European Common Market," Joyce explained. "I'm letting them use Hilbre as a temporary warehouse until they can find something better."

"I'm inside the Arctic Circle," Stagg persisted, "and I'm getting married again."

Joyce frowned and picked at a thread on her black track suit.

"What's her name?" She asked.

"Kyllikki. I met her in a place called Porvoo."

"Do you love her?"

"Yes."

"That's all right then."

Stagg went on to tell his mother that he was 'phoning from a small settlement of Skolt Lapps called Ivalo on Lake Inart.

"I want you to come to the wedding," he added.

"Can Moira come?"

"No."

"Why not?"

"I don't want people I don't like at my wedding, if that's all right with you."

There was a hiatus which was the space Joyce needed to absorb her son's back-handed compliment. After all, he did want *her* there.

"What have you been thinking about all this time you've been away?" she asked eventually. "I've been wondering."

"Well," Stagg answered, his mood more forthcoming by the minute as he tangled with his mother's mind once again. "I've been driving around a lot by myself."

"Not all the time by yourself," Joyce came back at him tartly, then adjusted her tone so that he would not pick up any censure. "What I'm trying to find out, son, is what's been going through your head."

"Only feelings," he said.

"No thoughts?"

176

"Not that you could bless with the name."

Joyce saw how pink the underside of her fingernails had become with the tension of her grip on the receiver. She relaxed and flexed her arm, then stiffened up again as she spoke.

"Have you had any feelings about me?" she asked fearfully.

"Plenty."

"I hope they weren't too harsh."

Stagg leant his forehead against the wooden wall of the telephone booth. A foot below where his brow touched was a dark, greasy mark where Lapps who had been smitten by similar moments of thoughtfulness had also rested their brain-boxes.

"I've never had a harsh thought about you, or a harsh feeling," he said. "You're my mother."

"And a friend, I hope?"

"Yes, a friend sometimes but mainly my mother."

Joyce experienced a stab of disappointment but she quelled her desire to pursue the point.

"Where do we go from here, then?" she said lightly. "You'd better let me know what I've got to do. I'll have to get myself ready for the journey."

By the time that Stagg had given his mother full travel instructions: a 'plane to Helsinki, then a train to Oulu on the north coast of the Gulf of Bothnia, which would involve a few changes, then another train to Kemi and Ravaniemi, the end of the line, followed by a hundred mile taxi journey over the tundra, Mrs Hankinson had returned with all Stagg's business messages.

"How much luggage will I need?" Joyce asked. "Is it a posh wedding or a registry office?"

Stagg told her that his marriage would be solemnised in a temple of the Sames religion.

"Say that again, please."

"It's what the Lapps call themselves. They say that they're the Sames. It's the Swedes who started calling them the Lapps."

Joyce grimaced at Mrs Hankinson and covered up the mouthpiece.

"Malcolm's got so much to tell me," she whispered. "He's fine.

All that time I've been imagining he's angry with me and there was no need."

Mrs Hankinson laid a list of Stagg's messages beside the telephone and sat down, thigh to thigh, with Joyce, her ears straining.

"Now, tell me about this girl you've got," Joyce said, her eyebrows raised at Mrs Hankinson who immediately leant forward.

"She's a soprano," Stagg shouted as the line faded after a long echo off the satellite-bounce, "Are you still there?"

"I'm here, son," Joyce replied. "I can hear you as if you were in the next room."

"I want you here by next Wednesday. Can you manage that?" Stagg bellowed, his voice filling the cubicle in the trading store where the fishermen were drinking beer before going out on the lake in the unending daylight of the far northern summer. "Do you think you'll have any problems getting here?"

Joyce assured him that she could see no reason why she should not be able to get to Lapland during the next five days. Stagg insisted on going through the travel directions once again, then asked her to bring his dark pin-stripe suit and a pair of black lace-up shoes which he usually wore with it. When he had finished, Joyce began to pass on his messages which he cut short, saying that he had no intention of thinking about anything but his fourth marriage for the next three months at least.

"Do you know what you're doing, son?" Joyce put it to him in the kindest voice she could conjure. "I hope it's not just the heat of the moment."

"Up here they value the heat of any moment they can get," Stagg replied, his voice now ringing out with the starry echo of the satellite. "You'll get along with her, I guarantee it. She's marvellous."

"When I get to this place Ivalo, where do I find you?" Joyce asked, anxious to suppress any further praise of the stranger.

Stagg laughed into the mouthpiece. As he looked out of the grimy store window he could see miles in every direction over the tundra.

"I'll know you're coming, Ma," he replied. "Don't you worry about that. Before I go, tell me, do you think you'll be all right travelling on your own? It's a long way for someone your age."

"It's only having to change trains which flummoxes me sometimes," Joyce answered airily. "But I expect it will all go like
clockwork once I get moving."

"Well," he said, "I'm proud that I can ask you to do this for me. It
wouldn't be right for you not to be here when I get wed."

"That's music to my ears, son," she replied, her heart high. "I
won't let you down. After all, I've been at all your other weddings.
Why shouldn't I be at this one?"

Joyce checked the route of her proposed journey in the atlas and
noticed how close Finland was to Estonia, so she rang Arvo in
Tallinn and asked him if he would like to accompany her to
Malcolm's wedding, thinking that he might enjoy the break from
his troubles. Arvo immediately agreed and crossed the Gulf of
Finland by ship to meet Joyce in Helsinki where they caught the
train to go north. Arvo was in much better shape than the last time
they had met. As a reformed character in all ways, political, moral
and dietary, he had begun to flourish, managing his sons' rock
group in recent tours of Estonia, Latvia and Lithuania. He had used
his trip to join Joyce as an opportunity to arrange meetings with
Finnish, Swedish and Norwegian agencies which had shown initial
interest in securing The Slavic Scourge for concert circuits, also he
hoped Joyce might work to help him break into the British market,
then, from there, launch an attack on America, an ambition dear to
his heart.

"The thing about Estonian rock," he said to her as the train pulled
out of Kemi station on the last leg of their rail journey from Helsinki
to Ravaniemi, "is that you can detect the reverberations of future
political and economic structures in it. It's all to do with expressing
the energy of the population and letting it blaze up in front of an
audience like a fire."

"But how can anyone trust a thing which happens so quickly?"
Joyce asked him seriously. "I'm used to people having to work hard
and long for what they want. Years! Then you come along, Arvo:
one moment you're on your last legs, very pessimistic and

depressed, then, a couple of months later, you're on top of everything and the past's forgotten. I can't help thinking that this might be a flash in the pan."

Arvo assured her that this was the pace of the new Europe, as it had been the pace of America when it had been the New World.

"It's all to do with time," he stated, unfastening his in-trip courtesy lunch, "that was the big confidence trick of the historical past. Everyone was told that success took a long time. If you wanted something it would take years. Apprenticeships, Studies. Degrees. The old Soviet government and its five-year plans, seven-year plans, hundred-year plans! But that was all a falsehood designed to suppress the ambitions and aspirations of ordinary people. Changes which happen too quickly unsettle our masters. They get nervous that they can be whipped out of power at the same high speed."

Joyce pondered, then said: "What have I been waiting for? I've no idea."

"Ah," Arvo murmured, spearing a piece of salami with his plastic fork. "You were being loyal to the dead. There is nothing to be ashamed of in that. But it can put the brakes on your life."

The taxi ride over the tundra was in a long-wheelbase pick-up driven by an old Lapp with one eye who had fish-hooks all down the front of his tartan lumberjacket. He spoke no English and drove the rigidly sprung vehicle at tremendous pace over the rough parts of the road, drawing protests from Arvo who was attempting to cushion Joyce from the shocks.

"He's only doing his best," Joyce assured him. "Perhaps he knows that we might be late. A wedding like this will be talked about all over the place, I should think."

"No, it's not that," Arvo contradicted her kindly. "It's because this man hasn't seen the night for a long time. The sun never goes down here during the summer months and it drives them mad. Many of them drink themselves stupid because of it, others go into a kind of trance. I think this old boy has managed both."

"No night? It never gets dark?" Joyce asked from under Arvo's arm where he was holding her.

"The Land of the Midnight Sun," he said with a sardonic chuckle, "where sleep is impossible, and waking up out of the question. What better place for your son to get married for the fourth time?"

Chapter Fourteen

When the Land Rover arrived at Ravaniemi, Stagg was waiting by the roadside in his car, his arm hanging out of the window with a cigarette. Joyce sat bolt upright as she caught sight of him and shouted to the driver to stop. When she climbed out of the Land Rover Stagg threw the cigarette away, got slowly out of the car, stood at attention, his eyes fixed on a point above the horizon, and told his mother that he had been jilted. His bride-to-be had turned out to be a woman of peculiar values who had started their affair and agreed to marry solely in order to get him to drive her from Porvoo to Ivalo to see her parents. "Sorry you've had a wasted journey, Ma," Stagg said. "D'you mind if we go straight back to Ravaniemi? I've had enough of this place to last me a lifetime. It's so primitive."

"You remember Arvo, don't you?" Joyce said, leaning against the Land Rover as her breath began to fail. "He's changed so much that you mightn't recognise him." She groped in her handbag for her Ventolin inhaler but recalled that it was finished before she could find it.

Stagg saw her fighting for breath and went to her side, putting an arm around her. "I thought you had this under control?" he said.

"I have," she gasped. "This is the first trouble I've had with my breathing since you left home. Maybe it's your disappointment's done it."

Stagg put his mother into his car with Arvo and the luggage then drove at speed to the small hospital on the naked shores of Lake Inart. It was empty of patients but the entire staff was on duty, playing cards. Joyce immediately became the centre of attention and within an hour a tall, gangling young doctor who possessed a pair of very long Neanderthal ears had told Stagg that his mother was suffering from exhaustion which had triggered off an attack of chronic bronchitis. She would have to stay in hospital to get her strength back and any journey home would need to be properly planned so that she did not get too tired. Fortunately, she had come to a hospital where she would get the best care as the area around Lake Inart was notorious for bronchial infections and an expertise in treating them had been built up over the years. In every respect Stagg's mother had been lucky to fall ill where she had.

"But your mother is too old to be cured," the doctor informed Stagg, "and her lungs have suffered from a lifetime of smoking cigarettes called . . . " Here he consulted his notes. "Capstan Full Strength in the brown packet. Coffin nails. You know this brand?"

Stagg nodded heavily.

"The important thing is that your mother must never catch a cold," the doctor went on, pulling at the base of his lobeless, hairy bacon-rasher ears, "and that she should never become too fatigued. Who allowed her to take this journey? From England to Lapland by 'plane and train! So foolhardy."

Stagg confessed that it was his fault and explained the reason. The young doctor had already heard the story about Kyllikki's gulling of her old English lover, as had everyone in the Lapp community.

"You have been playing with your mother's life," the doctor said, ticking him off. "Your mother is frail. Her life must be sedentary from now on. No shocks. Not too much excitement."

Stagg asked if the doctor would mind telling that to the patient.

"I've already done so," the doctor replied. "She agrees with everything I said. If you had not made her come on a wild goose chase, as she calls it, she would never have ended up in such bad shape. Have you any conscience? You'll have to pay for all this treatment, you know? This hospital is for the local people, not tourists."

Stagg sat with legs crossed, one elbow on a glass-topped cabinet, while the doctor listed the medication and treatment which his mother needed. It was a long list involving a nebuliser, an oral course of steroids and antibiotics, and a bedside drip of amino-phylline.

"I cannot release her for at least ten days," the doctor said after he had completed his account. "As I look at this I would guess that it will cost you the equivalent of half my annual salary."

That evening Stagg went to visit his mother and found her lying with the nebuliser over her face, inhaling a steamy mist. Arvo sat beside her holding her hand and reading a magazine. Stagg told Arvo that he had arranged somewhere for them both to stay but only one room had been available so they would have to share. Arvo nodded and released Joyce's hand, closed the magazine and excused himself. An hour later he had not returned. When Stagg made enquiries he was told that the Estonian ex-editor had left the hospital with his case and got a lift with a delivery lorry which was going back to Ravaniemi that night.

"What a shit!" Stagg raged after he had told his mother the news. "You see how much he's changed! Always the opportunist."

"I told him to go," Joyce whispered. "He's got things to do and this business is just you and me, Malcolm. It's not something for outsiders."

Joyce's recovery was much quicker than had been anticipated but she had to remain in the hospital for the full ten days in order to be weaned off the steroids. By that time Stagg had arranged for an air ambulance with a pressurised cabin to fly them both back to Heathrow. The initial arrangement had, in obedience to the doctor's instructions, been a car journey in easy stages, then a sea voyage from Helsinki to Harwich via Travemünde and Hamburg, but Joyce had said that she wanted to get back home to Hilbre quickly, even if it meant taking a risk going by air. So Stagg was forced to sell his car for half its value to a Lapp and hire a jet. As he sat gloomily in the air-ambulance and looked at the life-saving apparatus around him he reflected that he might need some of it himself when he totted up the total cost of his aborted marriage. But, he decided, it would be worth it if he got his mother back all in one piece and this proved to be the case. Except for five minutes use of the oxygen equipment during the six-hour flight, Joyce needed no relief treatment and took the trip well. When they got back to Hilbre at four in the afternoon she immediately went to bed and slept for twelve hours.

As for Stagg himself — he was in turmoil. His foolishness, his romantic illusions, his inability to read human character, caught up with him and savaged his soul. Mrs Hankinson tip-toed around him as she went about her duties, her saucered eyes always wide open as if in childish amazement that one man could make so many mistakes. It was she who took Joyce's meals up to her room and ushered the local doctor back and forth, smoothly adopting the positions of matron, nurse and housekeeper while Stagg was locked in silent, but internally violent self-recriminations, culling shapes and forms out of deep, swirling melancholies as his mind began to work again within his calling.

Then, through the grimness and unhappiness came a saving light. It was revealed to him what he should do. As soon as he had made sure that he understood the full meaning and implication of his own thought, he ascended the eastern tower and went to his mother's bedroom, taking a seat in a rosewood armchair which was shaped like the Prince of Wales' feathers. His mother was asleep so he waited, his eyes fixed on her face. She was without her dentures — a sight which he had never seen before. Both repelled and touched by the onrush of age which the toothlessness brought on, he fancied that he glimpsed great façades in the discernible shape of her skull beneath the drawn skin. While he struggled with the horror of his imagination, his mother opened her eyes, immediately aware of his gaze.

"I'm not going to wear my teeth any more," she said, sitting up. "I've been a vain woman."

"Never," Stagg replied, his mind bringing forth a memory of his mother coming down the stairs dressed up to go to a dance with an admirer. Stagg had been seven years old but he could recall every detail — the shape of her ear-rings, the way that she had worn her hair. He had waited for months to hear her say that she was going to marry the man. Why else would she have made herself so beautiful? But, like others who had sought her, the man had failed. Stagg had been amazed that nothing should come of such an outburst of unusual loveliness.

"When I was a girl my two front teeth stuck out a bit," Joyce told him chattily. "Not much, but enough to be noticeable. When your father joined the Army and went away I had my front teeth taken out under the National Health and got a pair of false ones so I could have a perfect smile. When he came home on leave and I went to meet him at the station he went mad and nearly hit me. 'Bugger Hollywood,' he kept saying all the way home. 'I loved those teeth like they were.'"

Stagg was upset by the story. He could see the girl in front of a mirror with her front teeth missing: it was a neo-classical portal, a marble gate into darkness. He closed his eyes.

"Lots of people had their teeth out because it was free," he heard himself say. "They thought it was something for nothing."

"What fools we all were," Joyce cackled. "All that pain."

Stagg opened his eyes and got out of the chair, then stood at the end of the bed. To do this he had to step up on a pile of prayer-mats which Ali and Yasouf had bequeathed to Joyce after the failure of their business in England and subsequent return to Tunisia.

"I'm going to sell Hilbre," he announced.

Joyce squinted up at him. He was so tall that even with the foot of the bed cutting him off at the knee, he seemed to be a holy, looming presence, his great head framed in the heavens.

"What's given you that idea?" she asked him.

"I've grown out of it. I'm not the same person who designed it. Sometimes I feel it holding me back." He sat down on the bed, swiftly telescoping his body to half its length in one rapid move. "I'll buy a house for you — and you can choose for yourself."

Joyce was short of something to say. As she looked around the high room and saw the clouds shifting the light over the pink and yellow banded walls she suddenly felt protective.

"This is my home," she whispered. "I haven't got the strength to leave it now."

Stagg got to his feet in pained wonderment.

"How can you say that," he protested. "You've always said that you hate the place!"

Joyce spent some time choosing her words. She knew that she had a brief future. Much of her time of late had been spent in serious meditation.

"I've started to understand what you were getting at when you designed it, son," she told him. "There's a lot of thought has gone into this house."

Stagg bowed his head. From his large brown eyes, shielded by fierce brows, he beamed a stare at his mother. Was she making a compromise out of fear? Had her spirit gone?

"You really mean that?" he asked her. "You feel comfortable here now?"

Joyce nodded. There was a strange, enlightening pause, then she said, "I'd prefer to stay." And that was the end of it.

With Mrs Hankinson's help, Stagg reassumed his life as an architect, moving around the world, spending his days in his work-suite or explaining his ideas to clients of all nations, earning money, losing some contracts, winning others. He was free to do this because his mother was at peace, cared for by her friend. Joyce's discovery of the meaning within Hilbre, its staggishness, was recuperative, providing entertainment and stimulation to fill her days. He was away from Hilbre a great deal but when he returned each time, he found his mother rested and at ease, still reading, still aspiring, but with a new distance between herself and her old ambitions. She would not admit that she had given them up but the pressure to fulfill them had diminished — or, at least, been put into a longer perspective.

These were better days for Stagg. His vision became more open and flexible, permitting new energies to flow. Notebooks were filled, boredom became a stranger, his mind consistently moving forward, making, making, abandoning old ground, rolling up time-stained documents, clearing desks and drawing-tables, his powers elbowing aside all obstructions and junk from the past. When he looked at what he was designing and set it against his old work — sometimes it was only a short distance away, standing there in his personal ziggurat of history, built, indestructable it seemed — he thought that two completely different men had dreamed up the ideas for two such opposite designs. But there he was, himself — intact.

The following March — after a quiet Christmas and New Year at Hilbre, his only revels being with friends in London and abroad during his comings and goings — he was in Toronto when he heard news of serious flooding on the Norfolk coast during the high spring tides. When he rang the house he discovered that the number was unobtainable, as was that of Mrs Hankinson at home. Within two hours he was on a flight to London.

He arrived at the inland limit of the great inundation at three o'clock in the morning. The road was barricaded and he was still two miles from Hilbre. When he got out of his car the water came above his ankles. There was no one around, no light, no house, so he walked along the road, keeping to the middle of the distance between the hedges, the cold brine climbing higher and higher up his long legs as he progressed. By the time that he had waded half a mile the water was up to his crutch.

Ahead of him he saw, by moonlight, a rowing boat tied to a railing outside a deserted bungalow. He splashed over and discovered that it was full of water, with a canoe paddle fastened to a small outboard motor. He went up to the bungalow and found a dustbin, emptied the contents into the water and used it to take the bulk of the water out of the rowing boat, then tried to start the outboard motor and failed. He took the heavy motor off and propped it up in the porch of the bungalow.

Sat in the back of the rowing boat, only able to make slow strokes with the paddle across the width, he moved the craft along the flooded road. It took him three hours to get to the gates of Hilbre and by then the sun was up and he could see his house standing in a huge sheet of water which extended to the sea.

Exhausted, soaked to the skin, terrified of what he might find, he found time and need in himself to admire the effect of the structure standing upon its own reflection, doubling its horned mass. Gulls were sailing over his gardens. The trees, in their winter bareness, hung over their self-images, some beginning to green. As he paddled laboriously towards the front door he saw a dead sheep. This shrivelled his excitement and ushered back his fear.

When he reached the house and entered he began shouting for his mother but there was no reply. The water was up to his chest and known household objects bobbed under his nose as he waded along the comma-shaped corridor towards the eastern tower. As he dragged himself up the stairs and left the water below him he heard the sound that the sea made inside the shape which he had created; a low, surreptitious laugh from a sly mouth.

The door of his mother's bedroom was shut. It had always been his instinct to knock before entering any private domain, but he did so with all the force of a god this time, thundering for access.

"Come in," he heard her call. "It's not locked."

She was sitting up in bed. Canned food was stacked on the floor and there was a sliced loaf, some margarine and a large piece of yellow cheese on a tray. An electric kettle, tea-bags and milk stood on the bedside table.

"Oh, you're back," she said. "I thought you might be Moira but then I said to myself — surely she wouldn't knock that hard."

Stagg had no words for what he was feeling. He was glad when his mother leant over and switched on the electric kettle, abbreviating the ringing pause between them.

"Don't ask me how this thing is still working," she said, smiling and showing Stagg that she had her teeth in, "but it is."

Stagg found his voice. As he began to speak, his mother instructed him to go into the bathroom and take off his wet clothes. He obeyed and returned clad in a voluminous pink bath-towel with tropical birds on it and started again, his indignation rising.

"Has anyone been to help you?" he demanded, watching the steam rise from the spout of the kettle. "They should have."

"Oh, yes. They've been here by the boat-load," Joyce replied.

"So why haven't you been moved out?"

"What was the point of going somewhere else? I knew the water would go down. I was safe up here." She put two tea-bags into cups and poured water over them from the magic kettle. "There was no need to make a fuss," she continued. "This house was never going to be covered by the sea."

"Did they ask you to leave?"

"Yes."

"And you refused?"

"Looks like it, doesn't it?"

Stagg accepted the hot tea and sat hunched over it, looking out over the submerged garden. A police launch cruised over from behind a stand of Chinese poplars and he recognised the figure of Mrs Hankinson standing in the stern.

"Here they are again," Joyce said. "Some people never give up."

The water went down over the next five days and the sea retreated to its old territories. As if to apologise, the sun began to shine and the temperature rose. Stagg supervised the repair and drying-out of the house, salvaging all he could, most of his attention going to his damaged work-suite, drawings and documents. Meanwhile, his mother obstinately remained in her tower, sulking because Stagg had forbidden her to assist with the business of reclamation in case she might over-exert herself. He had the sense to point out to her that, for her own sake, she should get out of the area until the level of dampness had reduced — maybe to go up to see Cissy in Liverpool or stay with some of his friends in London — but she would not go.

"This is my place," she told him. "I like my own bed."

The actual time and labour it took to completely rehabilitate Hilbre put Stagg's awareness of his mother's presence into the background. Not that he forgot her — every day he solicitously visited the tower — but there was something mechanical in his concern. Her will was now so strong that he could not imagine making a breach in it. She had taken a decision and they would both have to abide by its rulings.

The good weather lasted for the whole of April and May. One morning, when the end of the work on the house was in sight, he went up for his early visit, having fallen into a routine of three daily, and found his mother laid back on the pillows, her eyes bulging, her lips blue, battling for breath. When she saw him she feebly waved a hand at her bedside drawer, obviously too weak to reach. Stagg opened it and passed over the Ventolin inhaler but she did not have the strength to use it so he had to put it in her mouth and trigger it himself.

Unbidden and atrocious, an image reared up in his mind: he had shot his mother. The horror of this imagining was so powerful that it made him cry out.

The inhaler gave her little relief so he called the doctor who came within the hour and had Joyce immediately taken to hospital in Great Yarmouth. Stagg was advised that he had no need to accompany her and when he rang to enquire about her condition he was told by a ward sister that his mother was comfortable. That evening he visited her and she was better. Within three days she had been discharged and was back at Hilbre.

A week later he was in his work-suite when Mrs Hankinson rang through from the eastern tower and asked him to hurry over. When he got there he found his mother in the throes of another severe attack of breathlessness. The inhaler had proved useless and Mrs Hankinson was distraught. Stagg sent her from the room and took his mother in his arms, crying aloud: "I can't bear to see you suffering like this."

The doctor came and gave her treatment but he did not bother to send her to hospital. The next morning Stagg was in the kitchen when his mother entered and stood by the sink. She was very pale, her hair sticking to her forehead, and her lips were moving. As Stagg shepherded her back to her bedroom he heard her saying the opening words of the Lord's Prayer. He had never heard her pray before.

"You'll be all right," he said through his numbed mouth.

"I'm desperate for sleep," she whispered.

He could see how weak she was. She had not eaten for twenty-four hours. The doctor had given her sachets of mineral salts essential to life which she was supposed to take regularly. He mixed one of them with water for her once she was back in bed, but she vomited it up.

"Good old Malcolm," she said. "Always a tryer."

When he called the doctor he was told that the man was now on holiday and the locum would come as soon as possible. When Stagg opened the door he found a lovely young woman on the step, golden hair trussed up in a shimmering steeple, her eyes so bright that they blinded him.

"I think my mother has decided to die," he heard himself say.

"Well, we can't have that, can we?" the vision replied, stepping past him, her beauty brushing the very air he breathed. "That's silly."

"You don't know her," Stagg said, opening the doors of the lift. "She can do it. It's all my fault for breaking down in front of her."

When the doctor entered the room Stagg was behind her, looking over the top of her shining, tumbling hair. He saw his mother laid back on the pillows, her mouth open, her hair bedraggled, her eyes as sightless as the stones. One look was enough. He turned, swearing never to see her dead again.

"I'm sorry, Mr Stagg," the locum said, "but your mother has passed away. Don't blame yourself. Your mother died quite naturally, not because she wanted to."

Stagg left the room, his long legs stiff and awkward beneath him as he stumped down the curving corridor of his brain.